A 4seasonshelf publication
Copyright 2026 N.G. Swett

Novel, images & book design by N.G. Swett

Illustrated paperback
ISBN: 979-8-9893342-3-0

For a complimentary page of book discussion questions, contact info and more, please visit

4seasonshelf.com

For generations to come

"What seems today inconceivable will appear one day, from a higher stand point, quite simple and harmonious." ~ Max Planck

Table of Contents

The Clerk and the Ink Drinker in the Outer Lands Mission

Part I: Spring

Chapter 1: Bridge to the Future?

I'm heading out to pick up takeout for dinner, and I have to say, I'm feeling better already.

I just had my weekly televisit with my Territorial Specialist ("TS") -- by satellite. I'm finally done talking. I'm taking action.

I exit my apartment building and head to the avenue. On the sidewalk, I'm alert.

Before TS, I had Bob, my ex-therapist. Over time, he picked up on a few of my sore points, zeroed in on them, urged me to talk more, and I did.

Each week, we reopened the wound. Just when it scabbed up, it was time to open it up again.

Bob himself was a big talker, a natural. Unfortunately he went off into his favorite subjects a lot -- sports and boating. Sometimes I had to bring him back to why I was there.

My notions about the significance of the number 50 are simply magical thinking, he'd say again and again in front of his wall of advanced degrees. What it really means, he'd say, is I'm stuck on something that needs to be reckoned with so I can find a bridge to the future.

What does he know? I mean, what does he really know? What does anyone know? Why do I have to relive things to get some relief?

Why are all these sightings of 50 a sign of insanity? He thinks wearing official merch during a game helps his team win. He can have his but I can't have mine?

Not to beat a dead horse, but what about handing him my 50-dollar co-pay at the 50-minute mark of every session?

For Bob, everything circled back to my childhood, an enriching subject for sure, but for whom? I want to get beyond fairytales. I want to fulfill my own destiny, and time is running

out. There's no time for the scenic journey down
memory lane that Bob wanted me to take him on.

Bob questioned my statement, he said, "Time
is running out?"

He's like so many who are blissfully unaware
of endings. I'm closer to the end now than the
beginning. It's not a matter of if but when and
how. And then there are current events. It seems
the end of the world is also coming.

In the end, running out of lifetime mental
health bennies was the best thing that could
have happened to me. Without Bob's sad green
couch and his reality checks, my encounters and
obsession with the number 50 did not go away.
I gave into them. I followed to see where they'd
take me.

That's how I found a whole new kind of help,
the Odyssey Rescue Group (the Org). Now I'm
getting somewhere. When events reach a tipping
point, the Org will evacuate me. The Org gets it.

The first time I spoke with TS was within
minutes of dialing the hotline number. I kept
seeing the ad on the train, "extraordinary travel
for catastrophic times." I thought why not. The
dispatcher patched me right over to TS.

I described to him exactly what the number
50 was doing to me. I know this is a crazy
thing to say, but the universe is telegraphing
an important message on a tectonic scale. The

golden anniversaries, the 50-year milestones and retrospectives, are points on a curve. In my mind they form a huge 50-year wave. I've just been unable to decipher its message.

The first time we spoke, TS said, "The number 50? Yes, numbers can be highly significant, and we need people like you, people who can spot patterns, to help us gather intel."

I get into the flow of pedestians heading my way on the sidewalk. I called in my order right after I got off the televisit with TS. As I look at faces coming toward me on the sidewalk, many look stressed, sad, or hidden. Only children don't know what is happening as they cling to their caregivers.

Almost to Jin Hung's for my takeout, I see a big gold banner hanging from the front of the museum for a 50-year retrospective. I know I've got to pop in.

I've looked into history, and there's a coherent pattern of massive upheaval every 50 years with the same themes. Each time is almost identical in size and shape to the wave before it, and the one before that. There are 100-year waves, too, and waves bigger than that. We're part of the waves. I've seen it in my dreams.

The Org is helping me.

I'll get points for the museum retrospective. When I relay to TS encounters with the number, he sends them up to the Org, which immediately deposits points into my wallet through its app. Deposits vibrate in my hand.

Earlier today, I told TS about three encounters. One was the Roman numeral L spotted on an old stone building. Another one was a 50 percent off sale on the notebooks I use for journaling. The third one, devastating big news, was how many years women had control over their own bodies before the right was taken away.

Very few see the scale of what we're facing. TS sees it. It will all be in our report.

Now that TS set things up with me and the Org, I have more peace of mind than I ever did with Bob.

I follow signs to the gallery dedicated to modernity and find the retrospective group show -- "works that set off a revolution." Wow, there's a buzz in the air, and my antenna goes right up.

I take in the show, thinking of TS. He'll appreciate my findings. He'll pass them up to the Org, which I've come to envision as a glimmering council that assembles in the skies on dark nights.

In the gallery, I type with my thumbs and check for typos before hitting SEND: "NEW DISPATCH 50-YR WAVE REPORT. POTENCY LEVEL: HIGH."

Art is potent.

I pocket my device and continue viewing the artworks, taking a dizzying circular view from the center of the room.

TS is top rate, he always takes my dispatches and helps me sort through the data and signals coming across. In truth, he's become my main connection in life. Whether it's late at night, after watching the news scroll across my screens, or after calmer morning epiphanies, TS is always there and always helpful, a real pro. Take it from me, a lifelong member of one of the world's oldest professions: Clerk. It's as important as it is thankless.

Many in my profession are on the front lines with the public, and we can't hold out much longer. Lately, people have been going around destroying everything, and no one stops them. It's so distressing. It's almost physically impossible to "let it go" when managing and protecting valuable assets has been my life's work.

My pocket vibrates. It's TS. "DISPATCH RECEIVED. STAND BY."

Together with TS, after detecting 50-year wave patterns, we've also seen that the wave is on the cusp of breaking. Everything will be thrown into chaos, even our most animating beliefs. There will be no firm ground to stand on.

I've been told what to expect. Events will reach a tipping point. We expect increasing instability, a cresting, a snapping sound like a gunshot, and a catastrophic cascade of events. There will be a wild, frothing undertow of chaos and destruction. A total clearing will take place, which will take time.

When it comes to waves, TS says the best place to be is on the inside front edge, so we've been working on locations and logistics.

As I stroll through the exhibit—the bold shapes and colors, the irreverence, rebellion and yes, revolution of a half century ago -- it all mirrors the times we're living in now. The future will be salvaged from the wreckage.

I step out of the gallery into a dark hallway to put my findings from the exhibit into a few brief words for the report to the Org.

I press SEND.

My hand buzzes almost immediately. It's TS.

"BEGIN PREPS; AWAIT EVAC INSTRUX."

"Got it," I tap, exiting the museum. It's go time.

I hurry, stopping only to pick up my combo platter because I'm starving. I'm in and out of Jin Hung's in no time.

Back in my apartment, I gobble down my food and pack my satchel. The news is on in the background. I'm half listening for the thing that will be the tipping point. The reason I'm only half listening is because I shouldn't be helping this new regime achieve its apocalyptic vision by paying attention. But I can't help it. Dinner, a beer, and the news are giving me a bad stomach.

I'm packed and ready to skedaddle. My assets, a tidy sum I tended over a lifetime for a day like today, is now with the Org for safe keeping. Their proprietary geo-political calculations drawing on cutting edge technology are sending me to one of their bases.

Approaching dawn, I still haven't heard back from TS. The night wears on, and I can't sleep.

I'm approaching my own kind of crash when I finally get the call before dawn. They're sending me on a vital mission to its Outer Lands territory with the Ink Drinker.

I pinch myself to see if I'm dreaming. The Outer Lands? I question that. TS assures me my case was run through their super smart system and this is where I'm to be sent. It's no mistake. He says my familiarity with the territory makes me an invaluable member of the team. I'll pick up on things others wouldn't. He suggests I try thinking of it as an adventure.

Well, I was planning to never go back there. Enriching territory for Bob, that's for sure. Of course, the Org is different, and if I can help the cause, then I should.

I go. Without emotion, I exit my building for the last time. My old life, such as it was, is over. My new one is a leap of faith. I do worry, of course, but the Org is my last best hope.

Chapter 2: The Mission

Hello there! I extend my hand to you, the Ink Drinker.

We shake hands.

I tell you this is my first mission with the Org and that I'm glad to do it with someone who's been on so many of these missions.

Piece of cake, you say. In and out. Beautiful day for a flight to the islands.

There's no time to waste. The sun is coming up. Standing at our plane on the runway as its tank fills, we go over our mission.

This is a reconnaissance mission to aid the Org in the construction of a bridge to the future. We're to drop off dispatches to the longest island in the Outer Lands territory and pick up intel to bring back. I'm taking notes for when we report back to base. There's an added instruction to take evasive measures in the event forces attempt to waylay progress.

We climb aboard and strap into a red Stearman Kaydet biplane with yellow wings. We secure our satchels of dispatches.

My device buzzes with points! TS set the app so that points will be added to our wallets automatically, locally, when we find anything significant. He'll no longer be the go-between.

Preparing for takeoff, I note that the plane really is a beauty. It's commonly used for training. Rugged! It's got a fixed tailwheel undercarriage and 2-bladed fixed pitch propeller. The sensation of points flowing into my wallet helps me feel that I'm on the right path.

I take deep breaths as I've been trained to do, inflating my chest with air. Conjure up a state of no fear, no doubt -- just faith -- and achieve the necessary lightness of being to fly. Liftoff!

Once off the ground, we gain altitude, and we

soar off on air currents. Wingspan over 32 feet, cruising speed of 96 miles per hour, 10,000 feet altitude in about 17 minutes!

We approach the Outer Lands Archipelago, the string of primordial islands forged when the Labrador Glacier met the mighty Atlantic Ocean during the Ice Age. See those dark green shapes like birthmarks lined with silver edges in the morning sunrise?

I check mission coordinates and look for the longest island. You tip toward it. We're to land on a road with double yellow lines that starts at the end of the island.

There! That's what we're looking for. We're soon on the final approach for a landing. There's turbulence as we descend. The dispatches we're carrying are heavy. I feel something very strongly. I feel fear. I feel doubt.

Let's stay on course, you say.

I can't do it.

Just like that, the double yellow lines come undone like a ribbon.

We veer back over the sea. The propellers freeze. We're forced to make a sea landing. In a terrifying moment, we skim across the water. We come to a stop and start to sink. We strap on the satchels of dispatches and get into the freezing cold water.

We escape the fuselage and swim toward the

beach. A wave gathers and gets bigger and bigger as it approaches shore, sweeping us up with it.

Approaching the top of the wave, I can see you on the wave right along with me. The waves behind us form a tight formation of evenly spaced high peaks, a coherent pattern of surf pulsing a message on a secret frequency.

I turn and face the beach just as the wave reaches its absolute peak. In a silent moment before it breaks ashore, I know with no small amount of horror what's about to happen. A loud crack sounds across the wave.

You signal in a down direction and drop into the wave's tunnel to ride the wave in like a real pro. When the wave roars alive, I'm paralyzed by fear. It hurls me down to the sandy bottom. Powerful waters pound me down in rough, roiling, blinding blasts of white undertow. I'm sucked under and knocked senseless. I can't get my footing. I can't breathe!

Thank heavens, the wave's grip weakens and releases me into a rapid stream that takes me ashore and drops me there.

I raise my bedraggled head. There you are! What a relief! As much as TS tried, there was nothing that could have prepared me for that. It's something you just have to get through.

I'm scraped up pretty bad, and even you seem bedraggled. We sit there blinking in the morning

sun, glad to be alive. If that wasn't a 50-year
wave, then I don't know what is.

It dawns on us that now we're stranded here.
Our return flight is washing ashore or sinking to
the bottom of the sea. How are we going to get off
of this island and back to base? It worries me.

All the more reason, you say, to help the Org
get that bridge built.

We have flown, swum, and finally crawled
ashore to this place. We have a mission to
complete and now also the question of how to get
back. This was supposed to be just a routine intel
mission, in and out.

Shh-shhhhah, shh-shhhhah, the surf says.

This place is so familiar and so beautiful, and
it's a great privilege to be here with you today.
Soft sand shifts under our feet, and everything
is in motion: the water, the sky, the air. I'm soon
intoxicated. Nothing hurts. If we have to be
stranded, then let us be stranded here on one of
the world's most beautiful islands.

I message TS but get no immediate reply.

I try again a few minutes later with no luck.

Maybe when the equipment dries out?

We walk hunched over, frankly, with our wet
satchels of dispatches on our backs. We follow
the edge of the sea. The high surf thunders, and a
line of random objects cast along the shore grabs
our attention -- large sun-bleached clam shells,

driftwood, smooth pebbles, flattened rocks, orange translucent seashells, a small blue plastic shovel, clumps of seaweed, ribbons of sea grass, exotic spiral shells.

The treasures lure me along like breadcrumbs on a path. I want to collect them all, but my satchel is already heavy.

But you, you're good! You spot a metal, diamond-shaped road sign riveted to a tall stake in the sand and head toward it.

We walk around to the road to read it. In highly visible black lettering on yellow paint, it reads DEAD END.

It's obvious that the road ends where the sea begins, so much so that I wonder aloud why the sign is necessary at all.

You nudge me, pointing to an island attached to the shore by an old stone and timber causeway. An estate sits on top. It's like a fortress, untouchable by the gods themselves.

"Wow," I say and put my face toward the sun and take a deep breath of that mist-infused salty air mixed with verdant sweetness. The faint scent is elusive, growing fainter the more I try to inhale it.

I look around, and you've made your way along the beach toward that island estate. I stop chasing the sea scent and catch up to you.

To ask for directions? There? We won't be met

with open arms. More like an armed guard.

Nevertheless, you stride directly into the challenge, and I try to keep up.

Chapter 3: One's Island Estate

From the estate's entrance gate, you and I undergo a dizzying transport into a stone corridor. The air is tense with hushed undertones and bursts of laughter that come through the walls and doors.

We're soon in a corner of a finely appointed room with a stranger who calls himself One.

We're not perceived by One or even by a fat orange cat with a collar that says Goliath.

"One does love to sleep in, aye, Golly?" One says to the cat. One stretches his arms out from beneath his covers and gazes out the large picture window. The cat lifts his head, utters a lazy meow, and puts his head back down again. "Just look at that glorious bright blue sky, that glorious deep blue sea cloaked in mist, just brimming with opportunity!"

It truly is a spectacular spring morning. Anyone can see the archipelago is one of the world's most powerfully beautiful places. One could lay there forever, waxing poetic, mesmerized, lulled into oblivion, but One claps his hands together and snaps out of it.

He quickly finds himself marooned in bed, however, buttoned down under a paisley duvet. He feels around the nightstand and lays his lands on a brass bell. He's about to ring it when he notices a man standing there.

"There you are, Steve, my goodness how stealthy you are!"

Tall, dark and handsome in a classic way, Steve's lithe movements are so inconspicuous that it's possible he only comes into focus when needed.

"Good morning, Sir," Steve says, checking his watch.

It's a gold quartz watch, perhaps a gift from his employer. Its inner workings keep the beat of the estate. I'm mesmerized by it. Inside, a mechanical force presses a quartz crystal, and the crystal responds by keeping a steady beat. It is a world class instrument.

I'm astounded by its magic, and my pockets vibrate with points. Can you feel that? The low vibration, the buzz, of points filling pockets?

One sits up to lean against the pillows that Steve props up. "Good man. Now that you're finally here, I can get the spring program in motion." One demonstrates the concept of a spring program with a singular, circular gesture that comes very close to Steve's face.

"Spring program, yes, Sir," Steve says, turning to intercept the breakfast cart from staff at the door.

One watches Steve with secret admiration as he brings the breakfast tray. Indeed, Steve is quite something. I suppose it's a prestigious position, to be close with someone who is obviously so important as One. I can feel it. It's a force that practically bends gravity in some spaces, but in this intimate setting, One is childlike. It is Steve who is powerful.

Having delivered One's tray, Steve stands nearby like a sentinel. He looks out the window. With sea and sky meeting at the horizon behind him, the man's profile exudes a calm confidence that grounds One.

Very soon, with Steve gazing out the window a moment too long, One's mood suffers a deficit. He clears his throat and says, "Ahem... Springtime doesn't have the same bounding optimism it once did, does it?"

Steve's attention returns. "Sir?"

"Robbed us of spring, that's what the tree huggers have done! It's all so unfair!" One clutches his blanket to his chest and continues on. "Here I am, awakening to a beautiful spring day, and how does One feel? Doomed!"

Steve soothes One's despair with another rearrangement of the bedding and a top-off of hot coffee (but not too hot!) with cream. One takes a swallow or two, then toys with his eggs, bacon, potatoes, toast, and jam.

"Ah, that's the ticket," One says. He is pleasantly occupied for several minutes by mastication, the leveraging of utensils, sipping, tooting, burping, and donations of a few tender morsels to Goliath.

Really, though, we can't help but watch the manservant as he allows himself another moment to gaze out the window in an absentminded way. He'd be the one to get directions from on how to get off the island and back to base, if only we could communicate with him somehow. Alas! We don't register with him whatsoever.

"Well I mean, there ought to be exceptions."

"Exceptions, Sir?"

"Yes, exceptions. I mean, ordinary people live their dreadful little lives, experience all the hardships, fall ill, and die all the time. It's expected. But for those of us who have achieved more in life, we ought to have better options than this doom and gloom!"

You and I exchange glances. Seeing that we're both amused, we shake our heads.

"Ah yes, I see," Steve says. "Interesting."

Finally, One signals with a small wave of his hand that the tray may be removed. One says, "I suppose the kids are either still asleep or off running around again?"

Steve nods. "Yes, Sir."

"Of course they are."

"And Gwendolyn, that witch, is occupied in her own affairs?"

Steve nods again, "Yes, Sir."

Here, One takes a moment to ruminate with a long, glum stare out the window. "Wives are not the answer, and neither are offspring. Not mine, anyway. You! Ha! You're more useful than my own flesh and blood. You may be a man of the people, but you have that unique ability to straddle multiple strata, from the highest to the lowest. The agility of your general skull, your resourcefulness, and of course undying loyalty. I can rely on you completely, and I want you to know I appreciate it."

"Of course, and thank you, Sir, for saying so," says Steve as he pulls back One's covers for him.

Goliath jumps down from the bed and pauses so close to us we think he might sense us after all.

"Shall I prepare your bath, Sir?"

"Yes, yes, yes. Goodness, I'm still half asleep," One says to Steve's back. When Steve returns to the room with a bathrobe, One continues. "Now that spring is here, it's time to reset, Steve."

"Re-set, Sir?"

"Yes, precisely. Put our Spring program into high gear."

The tub is half full before One kicks off his slippers. The level rises to the top as One slips in and gradually lays back. Bubbles tickle the back of his neck. Gleaming faucets keep the hot and steamy coming. Such a feeling! A good splash in the face extinguishes all doubts and refreshes One's thirst for life.

The feeling that all is quite well lasts through Steve's dressing, until One pulls away and says, "Enough with the infernal, eternal tucking and brushing!"

Steve gets him seated in the den and lights One's first cigarette of the day. With a sharp, deep first drag and purposeful exhale, words begin to form. One moves into a more philosophical, commercial line of thought.

"To summarize, winter is over, and it was excellent," One puffs away on his cigarette, flicking ashes in the general direction of the standing ashtray. "But now that spring is here, it's time to spring ahead, make some gains!"

"Indeed, Sir," Steve says. "Always cooking up something big."

"What we need is more," One says. "More of everything. The most. The best."

"Undoubtedly key, Sir."

"I intend to push the envelope, Steve. To do what has been done throughout the ages when new territories, new discoveries, new resources were needed: what I call 'expeditions'."

One can't say this with enough vim and verve from a seated position. He rises and raises an index finger into the air. "Steve, let's have a large sherry to brace ourselves for bold new explorations."

Steve clears his throat. "Hear! Hear! Sir!"

"It won't do, sitting and waiting for everything to be handed to us, like everyone else does, while the world disintegrates before our eyes. Be first. Be bold. Reap the rewards. Lay claim to uncharted -- and unregulated! -- territories, that's where the best things lie."

"Your sherry, Sir." Steve delivers an extra large sherry, Johnny-on-the-spot.

"We must train our sights away from the

ugly doomsday naysayers, the Chicken Littles, this dark portal of death that is the scientists' prognosis for our dear planet. Let us turn toward its polar opposite: the bright yonder. As I say, look to new horizons, into great untethered minds, new dimensions, new physics perhaps, the technological age, and whatnot. We must chart a course! Who knows, maybe find a way out before the end."

"Make things happen, Sir, that's the spirit."

Steve gets it!

This mutual admiration society gets peppier as more cigarettes and more booze are consumed, into heights so abstract and so unknown to us that it trails off into the ether, which is of no use to us in our current situation.

We have crash landed our plane into this terribly beautiful island with these wet dispatches, we don't know how we'll get back, and asking these two gents isn't panning out. Just as we're about to cut our losses, One says something that gets our attention.

"What about that infernal bridge, dammit!"

Did you hear that? He said bridge.

Okay, we're listening.

One continues, "I'd have thought by now that I could look out the window and see the thing rising in a gleaming arc from this island out over the sea, over to the mainland, opening up new

connections and opportunities! It's past time
we made that happen. Enough is enough from
the locals! If they're too small minded to see the
future, then we must build the thing whether
they want it or not."

Our hearts sink. This bridge we seek isn't even
a concept of a plan yet. One describes the bridge
as mere decor out his window, but a bridge takes
approvals, planning and construction.

"Yes, Sir, I can find out the status of the bridge
project, change tacks, get some wind behind it,"
Steve says.

"That's what I like to hear, Steve. It may take
a big push — and a shove or two. It'll all become
crystal clear in the hours and days to come," One
says, pacing the room to get the juices flowing.
"In the meantime, tell Cook I'll be having all of
the usual captains of industry and overseers,
attorneys and bean counters, along with some
of the most brilliant minds of our times, here for
meetings. Look smart, I say. Tip top. Stay alert."

"Yes, Sir. I will coordinate presently with staff.
Will there be anything else for now, Sir?"

"We're mobilizing, Steve. A pitcher of your
special, magical cocktail is what's needed. Up on
the terrace, I think, so we can take a broad view."

On the sunny southern side of the terrace,
Steve serves such a stupendous elixir that we can
taste it. One gulps his glass down with a fresh sea

breeze. He holds his glass out for a refill, already quite euphoric.

"Keep me informed of the bridge project, I want to see that move forward while our spring program, our great expedition into the unknown, takes shape. Let's move forward!" One strides with drink in hand to the shady leeward side of the terrace, with a view of his marina and yacht.

"Yes, Sir." Steve watches a white delivery van below at the gate. It's crossing from the estate to the island via the causeway. He checks his watch. A full moon still hangs in the blue sky, and a king tide laps the shore.

You and I are alerted by a flurry of points pouring into our wallets like a weak electric shock, as we, too, watch the delivery van.

One notices Steve's distraction and says, "Come on, feel like a drive?"

The color drains out of Steve's face.

Before going down to the garage, One takes an extra moment in the shade to finish the pitcher and consider how much has been accomplished before lunch time!

On a hunch, you and I decide to hitch a ride with the white delivery van. Before we go, I'm inspired to check my satchel for a parting gift and come up with only a damp dispatch with the title of "GLORY?" I slip it into One's jacket pocket and rush to catch up with you.

Chapter 4: The Club

The white delivery van, a non-descript ordinary van, whisks us to a country club. We come into the parking lot too fast for the likes of a burly young man crossing to the club house entrance. He is very -- very! -- mad. His back hunches, muscles pop out of his neck. His short cropped hair stands on end as he barks at the van driver.

Finally, the mad man has nothing left to say. As he walks away, he runs his hand from front to back over the top of his head, smoothing down his hair. By the time he gets up the walkway to the door, he has subdued his inner beast.

The clubhouse door is a grand portal. Thick vines form a deep archway of rich green ivy over heavy wooden doors. On pure instinct, we follow, slipping in as the doors close.

The dining room host escorts all three of us to a table of four distinguished men seated at the big picture window overlooking the grounds.

I snort, but luckily no one can hear me. Or see us.

Why am I snorting, you ask?

Well, look what they're wearing: three quarter pants, silly shoes, soft luxury fabrics, athleisure business attire. Ridiculous, especially the two older men, whose colorful garments rival the most extrarordinary creatures of nature. Compared to the gray drone of destruction happening where we come from, this is otherworldly.

Why don't I try again to get ahold of TS. Good idea. My device should be dry by now. I compose an S.O.S. to TS and hit SEND.

In the glare of the southern-facing window, the men look like rock statues set against a green lawn. They don't get up, but one by one they address the mad man, "Hey Earl."

Earl isn't dressed like a member, but he is dressed in his Sunday best. As he settles down at the table, we see that the club's decor harkens back to the tastes of robber barrons. From where they sit, club members literally experience the sun revolving around them from east to west. The classic club decor of wood paneling, leather, and carpeting doesn't acknowledge the moon landing.

No, the men are blissfully unaware of the planet spinning and hurtling through space toward obliteration, all of us together holding on for dear life. New physics? Einstein himself wouldn't have been admitted through the door, let alone his wild ideas.

I'm starting to think we're not going to advance our mission or find a way back from this place. I put down my satchel and open it to check for any clue. A single damp dispatch rises to the top. I know that it's meant to be delivered to these gents.

As I'm looking at it, a waitress comes to the table. The men exchange glances as the waitress takes drink orders.

"Thank you, gentlemen, I'll be right back with your drinks and to take your lunch orders," she says. She has a sweet little engagement ring on her finger.

"Thanks, Tammy," they say and watch her go. The two younger members exchange long looks of longing with each other, which Earl notices and joins in on with a low moan. The three share a little chuckle.

One by one, their desires turn to their stomachs. They peruse the menu and chat about the club.

When Tammy returns, she balances five tinkling drinks on a tray like a circus girl. She steps next to each man, twists and twirls herself to give each man his drink and a little individual attention.

She repeats back each man's lunch order, which significantly boosts each man's sense of himself.

Tammy says, standing erect, pen and pad poised, "John, filet mignon, rare, with another martini? Certainly. Thank you." Tammy turns twenty degrees to his right. "And Bob, for you, lamb chops well done with a cabernet?"

She goes all the way down the line, giving each member a view of her cleavage as she reaches over to take their menus. Tammy jots down veal parm, a cheeseburger and beers for the younger members, and for Earl breaded chicken strips with a beer.

Earl holds onto the menu an extra outrageous moment when it's his turn to give it back to Tammy, holding eye contact.

Over lunch, the members inquire with concern about Earl's family and how the farm is doing. Earl says the family's holding up, and so's the farm.

Good, good, good to hear, they say, shaking their heads. They say, "If there's anything we can do...."

Then, the four members have distracted side conversations about their health, trips, and new toys.

Leaning against the glass wall, looking on, and hearing nothing about any bridge, my doubts creep in again. We're here with these knuckleheads wasting our time when maybe we should have stayed with the van.

Ages and ages come and go of mindless, useless prattle before Tammy stops at the table to ask if she could interest anyone in dessert or another drink.

You and I, we'd like to hear the dessert menu, even if we can't have any.

"Earl?" the eldest member avers.

"What've ya got that's sweet?" Earl says intimately, looking her up and down until his eyes fall on her breasts and stay there.

"Actually, ahem!" says the second oldest member to Earl, glancing at his watch, "I apologize, Earl. Look at the time. It's tee time. I'm afraid we don't actually have the time today. Lunch is on me today, Tammy. Thank you."

Earl waves off dessert but keeps one arm draped over the back of his chair watching

Tammy go. The group gets up to leave. The older members say their goodbyes and head out to the green. I manage to tuck the dispatch titled "DISPENSATION?" into the oldest member's pants pocket.

The two younger members walk Earl out to the parking lot.

We trail along, looking for the van, but it's gone.

"Good to see you, Earl, glad you could join us," say the two members, one after the other.

"Sure thing. Always nice to rub elbows with the bigwigs," Earl says.

The men grin.

"What's the waitress's story? I'd like to get in touch with her."

"Whoa there, Earl," says one member. "You're gonna get us all in big trouble around here. Besides, that little gal's spoken for."

"Well that's a damn shame," Earl says.

"Now look, Earl, on a serious note, we've gotta ask you," says the other member. "What do you think of the highway extension and bridge they're proposing to build along your road there? You for it or against?"

We jolt. Our ears perk up. Bridge? Proposal to build? We lean in. Maybe we haven't lost the thread after all.

"Haven't given it much thought to be honest,"

Earl says.

"Well give it some thought. A big chunk of the land they'd need belongs to you and your family. Up to people like you in a large sense whether that bridge happens or not. It might be good for the town. It sure could be good for you."

"Yeah?"

"Yep. Your folks are getting older, you've got a lot on your shoulders especially with your brother laid up. You're spending all your time scratching a living off that big farm and collecting a little rent here and there. Now, if you sell off the land, you and your family would be able to relax the rest of your lives, enjoy yourselves a little. Get yourself a membership here. Lord knows, you deserve it."

"I wouldn't mind if that gal gave me lunch every damn day, that's for damn sure," Earl says, with a nod and a guffaw toward the dining room. "As for this bridge thing, I have no idea. I'll definitely look at that."

The members invite Earl to come by their offices anytime. They'd be happy to walk him through the details personally. He won't even have to read the plans.

Earl says, "Well, that would be a change of pace. Seems like all I do all day every day is get after people who don't seem to want to work for a living. My folks and my golden boy brother aren't

36

of much use any more, I do every damn thing
that needs doing."

"Exactly. Every year, you all need a bank
loan just to plant. No shame in that, most all the
farmers do. Spinning your wheels, not getting
anywhere. Year after year. But I can tell ya,
farmers selling their land are making out real
well, I can tell ya that for sure cause I done some
of the deals myself."

"Plus, lotta opportunity could be created for
everyone around here with this bridge. You cash
out, and a lot of new money flows in. It's a win-
win. Good for the whole town."

"Yeah?" Earl says. The three have drifted
over to his truck, a gold-striped C10 pickup, the
fiftieth anniversary edition.

Ho-ho! You and I each get an influx of points
for that beauty.

"There's gonna be some public hearings
coming up right after Labor Day," says one
member, pulling out his pocket calendar. "You
know how those are, especially these days. Would
be great for a real local to get up and say a few
words on the record as someone who actually has
standing as a property owner."

The other member adds, "Those of us who can
see the benefits can't be the only ones to speak
up. Local people want to hear from ordinary
local people. You're local as it gets. Your family's

sacrifice, your brother's being a wounded veteran and all, well, people have strong feelings for you in this town. There's too many locals who just don't seem to understand the potential of this thing, but I think you might. You don't even have to read the plan, which just puts everyone to sleep. I can just tell you right now, this bridge is your ticket to the easy life for sure. Don't need anyone to tell you otherwise or talk you out of your family's rights as landowners."

"Yeah, okay," Earl says with a wave. "I'll be in touch."

It seems like Earl feels there's been enough talk for one day. He turns and walks toward the cab, running his hand along his truck's smooth, shiny back before opening the door and climbing in.

It occurs to us that it's Earl who holds the key to the bridge now. We get in the truck before the door closes.

I run my eyes over the interior of the truck's cab. Its style and comfort show a love and consideration of the owner that is hard to come by in this world. The waitress would surely enjoy its bucket seats with full depth foam cushions, the center console, armrest, and sun visor. We do! We touch everything and deeply inhale that new car scent.

Earl turns the key, and the engine comes alive

with a roar, then purrs, waiting for Earl's next command. He puts it in gear and points the nose of the pickup out of the club and onto the Main Road.

Earl mutters as he drives.

"Those guys, with their little cups in the grass to tap their balls into. Spring's a hell of a time to be springing things on me. It's always something. What's it this time?"

Chapter 5: Earl Reckons

Earl stops at a small ranch-style house. It's on the same property as a large farmhouse. When he comes back out, he's changed from his Sunday best into jeans that sag from his belt buckle down to his boots. His gait is slow and assured as he walks back to the truck and climbs in. Behind his aviator sunglasses, his eyes scan for anything and anyone out of their God-given place. Earl is grouchy.

"What, it's supposed to be some kind of privilege to get called down to the club? All their bullshit..."

We bounce down his dusty driveway. He scratches his head as he pulls out onto a country road with double yellow lines. A sign says it's called Sumditch Avenue. We squint at the shiny bright paint reflecting the sun's rays.

"The bridge, that's what they want, that goddamn bridge," Earl says aloud. His palm hits the steering wheel. He's having an epiphany. "Son of a gun."

Earl turns onto a dirt road and pulls up to a small structure with a large tank outside. It's quiet now, but in the summer, the pump house's solitary metal inhabitant will devour diesel from the tank and send groundwater up and through the irrigation pipes. Water travels along their lengths to spinning sprinkler heads, which pulse out streams of water onto crops.

Earl gets out of his truck and steps over to one of the many rusted chemical drums. He pulls down his fly and relieves himself. "The future of this whole damn town is in my hands," he says with a chuckle and a grunt. Then, he strides inside the pump house.

You're about to follow him in but I grab your sleeve. Let's wait outside. I open my satchel to air out the dispatches, hoping to make the bag lighter. There's a dispatch for Earl in there with the title "GOD & COUNTRY?" I place it under his windshield. My satchel feels that much lighter.

Checking my device, there's no message from TS, but I note that the pump added points to my wallet.

Chapter 6: Unwelcome Visitor

Twenty minutes later, we're on our way again.

It's a jerky, bumpy ride with Earl at the wheel. When he swings his truck off the road at such high velocity, if you've ever seen something slide across the dash of a car and out the window, that's us.

We're flung past a big metal mailbox with DEMPSEY printed across the side. We sprawl onto a hill of fresh spring grass. To catch up with Earl, we amble up to a pebbled driveway. We follow his truck until it stops next to a white picket fence and a bed of colorful spring blooms.

Like fools, we stoop to inhale the scent of each fresh flower.

There are no other vehicles in the driveway, and Earl cuts the engine, taking a long look at the property. He whistles a high note, then switches to one low one.

He's about to leave when a car turns into the end of the driveway.

The car pulls up and stops. It's a big, beautiful, champagne-colored Buick Electra! Points gush into our wallets.

The car door opens, and the foot of a lady steps out. Her ankle is bare, and her foot is encased in a beautiful shoe that points her toes. One foot is followed by another. She stands in the driveway wearing form-hugging pink slacks and a tan bodysuit. She reaches in the back window for a shopping bag and doesn't even glance in the direction of Earl's truck.

She tiptoes gingerly on the pebbles to the gate of the picket fence. Once on the brick path to the porch, her gate is more strident. She steps up to the porch and opens the screen door, then the storm door, and steps inside. The screen door shuts behind her with a loud thwack, and she shuts the storm door, too.

A few minutes go by, and there's a quiet knock at the screen door. It's Earl.

We're tagging along. We're a bit unsure of where we're supposed to be, to be honest.

"Sorry to disturb you," Earl says when the lady opens the storm door. He looks in, thumbs hooked in his back pants pockets.

"Kevin's not here," she says and turns to walk away. "He's probably out back if you want him."

Hearing ice cubes jingling in a glass, we follow her into the kitchen. Oh my god, aren't they glorious? So cold we can see microcosms of ice air currents and swirling clear liquid in — what is that, ice tea? — ice tea! It's lightly sweetened, but you can still taste the bitterness of the tea mixed with the soft bitter juice from a slice of lemon at the top of the glass.

We hear something that sounds like the tap-tap-tapping of a woodpecker. No, it's Earl again, tapping his school ring against the screen door.

"Like I said, Kevin's probably out back."

"Putting pleasantries aside here for a second," Earl says, "I'm here on some business."

"That's why you should find Kevin."

"Since we're both right here... I'm sure Kevin's working hard. Who knows how long it would take me to track him down. Can't I just give you a tiny little message for him this once?"

"What is the message, Earrl?"

He likes the way she says the "r" in his name nice and slow. He takes a moment to appreciate it fully. "The bridge. Just tell Kevin I need to talk to him about the bridge."

"Got it, bridge, I'll tell him, bye." She turns again toward the kitchen.

"Whoa, whoa, listen, this concerns you, too, ya know."

"Here we go. Yeah? How's that, Earrl?" Her irritation is really showing. She steps toward the door, her arms crossed. For Earl, any reaction at all is plenty.

He leans in a little and speaks in a friendly, low voice, moving his hands into his front pockets and shakes his head. "Come on, Francesca, a woman like you? There's not much going on around here. You should be in the movies or something. This bridge is your ticket outta here."

Francesca lifts her chin, scowls at Earl in genuine disgusted amusement, and swings the door shut in his face.

He steps back, shaking his head.

You and I are on the other side of the door from Earl. We move toward the clinking glass of sweetened ice tea.

Francesca sits down with her glass. She rummages through the shopping bag on the chair next to hers. Yes, let's sit here for a minute at

Francesca's kitchen table having iced teas.

A man opens the back kitchen door and steps in.

Chapter 7: The Newlyweds

"Hey, baby," he says at the door, leaning over and removing his work boots.

"Hey," Francesca says, still looking through her shopping bag.

He is tall, lean and handsome. He wears a loose navy blue tee shirt with a chest pocket, jeans, and socks. He goes straight into the bathroom and washes his hands.

When he comes back, he kisses Francesca.

"Look at you, all dolled up and gorgeous," he says. "Oh, and a little shopping, too, I see."

"Had my hair done. What do you think?"

"Nice. Very nice."

"I'm starving," she says, standing.

"Me, too."

"Can you make us something?" she says, clasping her hands behind his neck.

"Me?" he says, pulling her closer.

"Kevin, I just walked in the door! Earl Butts was by. He wanted to talk to you, I told him to go round back, and being the creep he is, he insisted on talking to me anyway."

"Poor Earl, he always did rub girls the wrong way," Kevin says. "What did he want?"

" 'Poor Earl,' " Francesca says. "Well how nice you care so much about him, but what about me? I'm the one who had to have a whole conversation with him."

"You're the best, and you smell so nice," he says, pulling her in closer.

"Yeah and since I'm the one who had to deal with him, I think that you should make us a sandwich," she says, pouting.

Wow, she really means it. You and I have to applaud her. She may indeed be a star someday.

"Well, Mam," he says in his official deep voice, which he knows she can't resist, "While you've been sitting in the beauty parlor all morning making yourself so gorgeous, which we do appreciate, your hardworking husband has been out in the field, working. Shouldn't you make me a sandwich?"

"You make it sound like you're pulling the plow yourself," she says, walking over to the window. A tractor is parked outside the barn. She points to it like it's a game show grand prize and shakes out her beautiful mane. "You just sit up there and drive real slow, how hard can that be?"

"Well," he says, following her, "looks like both of us are just gonna have to go hungry." He goes and stands close to her at the counter and takes a deep breath of her perfumed hair. He gently kisses her ear, sending a current down her neck. He whispers, "Don't you love me?"

She leans her head back against the cabinet and sighs. A golden bracelet falls down her wrist as she moves a strand of hair out of her eyes.

He grazes his lips along her ear, to her full mouth, still cool and sweet from ice tea. He plants small kisses on her mouth until she nuzzles him away to her cheek.

He kisses her cheek and finds her mouth again, tilting her mouth up toward his. She starts to kiss him back, then pulls away to ask, "Where's your father?"

"Having his lunch next door with Grandma and Grandpa," Kevin whispers, kissing her neck and pulling her closer. "Just you and me here."

She raises her arms and runs her fingers through his fine hair. He looks down at the top of her breasts showing through her blouse. They kiss.

"Come on," he whispers, taking her hand. "Let's just forget about lunch and go upstairs."

Kevin leads Francesca by the hand. In the living room, she stumbles trying to kick off her shoes. He catches her, and they fall laughing onto the lush green carpet. Laying there at the foot of a floral print couch as if in a sunny meadow, they kiss playfully, then passionately, and then urgently. Garments are unsnapped, unbuttoned or pushed aside. Fabric rubs on the carpet and sends little sparks flying through Francesca's hair and fingers.

As beautiful as they are, the sparks are our cue to retreat back into the kitchen, give the lovers their privacy. We may not know where we're supposed to be, but it's not in there with them.

I rummage around in my satchel and pull out a dispatch with the title "TRUE LOVE?" I leave it pinned to the fridge with the magnet.

What does it mean?

I'm not sure, but my satchel is a bit lighter.

The couple shuts out everything else in the room, everything else in the house, everything else in the world. There's certainly no bridge to think about.

Soon, Kevin collapses into Francesca's hair, now a beautiful mess.

"Aw, Kevin, look at us," she says.

He helps her push strands of hair out of her face, leaning beside her on one elbow. "What do you mean?"

"I get back from the beauty parlor and in no time I'm lying on my back on the floor."

"Mmm, yes you are." He gently kisses her nose and forehead.

She looks up at their wedding photos, displayed in a row on the credenza. Her in her beautiful white gown, and him in his tuxedo and pine green bow tie and cummerbund, posing together. The farm behind them is like the grounds of a royal palace. "Come on," he says. "I'll make us a sandwich."

At the kitchen table, eating BLTs with iced tea, Francesca sits on Kevin's lap.

Kevin finishes his sandwich first, and while Francesca finishes hers, he caresses her. "So what did Earl have to say?"

"He's such a pig," she says. "He wants to talk to you about a bridge."

"OK."

"But he also had to be gross. He said a woman like me's going to waste around here."

"Hmm. Did he really?"

"Really. And that I should be in the movies."

"Well he's not wrong about that. I'll talk to him."

They don't say any more about it. When Francesca finishes eating, Kevin pats her on her bottom and kisses her behind her ear. "I should get back out there," he says. "I can't leave Dad to go it alone out there." He grabs a small cooler and opens the fridge.

A forlorn Francesca places their dishes in the sink then gazes out the window as he walks out the door and up the grassy hill toward the barn and the big handsome tractor chomping at the bit to plow through fresh spring fields.

We watch as Kevin stops before crossing the driveway to wait for an old Ford truck to come up to him. He leans over to talk to the elderly couple inside of it, and before long, they drive away as slowly as they came.

In the kitchen, the ice cubes are melting, and there's a little puddle under each iced tea glass. We watch the fissures crack.

The tractor starts up with a roar. We race up there.

Chapter 8: Spring Plow

When we get up to the Dempsey barn, we're rewarded with many, many points for two tractors, a 90-horsepower diesel John Deere 4020 and a "HiClear" 110-horsepower diesel Farmall 806.

How about a quick tractor ride through country fields, should we go?

Father and son fire up the engines. Kevin Jr remembers the cooler and hops off to get it. Faced with the choice of which tractor to ride on, we go with the one with the cooler.

Kevin's head is in the clouds as he bobs along behind his Dad, Kevin Sr, on the dirt farm road.

His Dad signals for him to take the field on the left while he goes further on. Kevin turns, and here we go!

Oh my! The first rough cut into a wintered, rested field! We wish we could bottle the scent.

Kevin Jr inhales deeply, too. Slow and steady Kevin goes, and we're in ecstasy. We're flush with points, and this country tractor ride is recharging my spirit. I'm not even thinking about our mission or how to get back.

Instead, I comment to you on the newlyweds. Kevin's obviously wild about Francesca, but let's face it: she doesn't seem like a farmer's wife. Everyone works hard on a farm. On top of everyday hard work, they've got the whims of Mother Nature to contend with, not to mention national farm policy, bankers, insurance, pests, fertilizers, water, and markets. Well, it's a lot. Look at Kevin Jr though. He isn't thinking about all that. He's thinking about her.

Well they're young, after all.

And what about Kevin himself? Is he cut out for farming? He's handsome and young and maybe a little wild at heart, a bit impractical choosing a wife who's no farmer's wife. Is his destiny neat rows of crops as far as the eye can see? Is he glad to see his whole future rolling out in four seasons over and over again until he dies?

Maybe, maybe not.

Ah, can you smell that? Think about it, this land belongs to him and his family.

Before long, Kevin will have a child, if Francesca gives him one. And then his child will belong here, plowing the fields in spring. His child will breathe that divine spring fragrance, too, taking that yearly leap of faith that tended seeds will grow into food.

Yes, a family farm is a special thing that's getting rarer all the time.

After a couple of rows, Kevin reaches down to the cooler. He fishes out a beer and pulls the tab. Its cold carbonated contents rush out, and he slurps it off the rim. He takes a few long gulps. The fragrance of the beer added to the fresh soil is a recipe for elation. You and I feel that.

Kevin cracks open another beer, and this time the effervescence causes two thoughts to pop into my head. One was Earl's message to the newlyweds about the bridge. The second was that the Dempseys also have a stake in it.

Unwittingly, out plowing with Kevin Jr, we've lost track of time and our mission. We're quite drunk on love, dirt, and beer. But when we hear Earl's truck roar down Sumditch Avenue, we snap out of our reverie and follow.

Chapter 9: Sumditch Avenue Crusader

We scramble to the farm across the way from the Dempsey farm, where Earl's truck is kicking up a cloud of dust in its driveway.

A wind chime signals a disruption of the peace to the old woman standing outside the barn working. Strands of twine blow off a workbench to the ground. The woman puts her hands on piles of weeds to keep them from blowing.

Her dog is up on all fours barking, fur raised. Earl has pulled all the way up to the barn in a manner the dog finds aggressive.

The old woman resumes placing clumps of bright yellow dandelions in a bucket. Her wide brimmed hat and a braid keep her wild gray hair out of her eyes, and a sweatshirt is tied around her waist.

Once Earl cuts the engine and the dust settles, peace returns. Migrant birds chatter and flit about, scoping out nesting materials, chasing each other around, and calling from the treetops. With skulls and breasts encased in flesh and guided by mysterious homing devices, some over great distances and at great peril, the migrants return to the region every year.

The dog stops barking and approaches the truck as Earl gets out in his own time. He walks up and stands in the barn's open doorway.

The woman says hello without interrupting her work. Her back warms in the sun as she makes a brew of rainwater, dandelions and quartz powder. Sprayed on plants, it will endow crops with the hardy weed's will to survive and the special properties of quartz.

You note that I seem to know a lot about this, and you're right I do. It's an occupational hazard of being the Clerk, having so much info at my fingertips.

"Well hello there Alexine," says Earl to the woman, adjusting his hat brim. "Been a while, thought I'd pay you a visit on this nice spring day." Earls pats his knee for the dog to come to him, says, "Hey Duke, come 'ere boy."

The dog stays put.

Earl pokes his head inside the barn. It's old but still pretty solid, like the woman herself.

"Nice to see you, Earl. Yep, been a while," Alexine says.

"I see you survived the winter," he says.

"Yep."

"Can't be getting any easier as time goes by." As they speak, Earl's eyes dart around the property, assessing it.

"Yes and no," she says. She ties a piece of burlap over the bucket with twine. She leaves it there and walks inside the barn.

Duke gets up, stretches, and moves slowly toward the barn door, sniffing at the dirt and watching Earl closely. If the dog senses us, he's not showing it. He does look our way a lot and holds his gaze, sniffing the air.

Alexine takes a rake down from a wall hook and grabs a folded tarp from a shelf. She places both in a wheelbarrow and wheels it out. She rolls out to the front yard and starts raking. Earl and the dog follow.

Alexine glances at Earl, who is surveying the front of the property. She sees the laundry list that he sees: the paint peeling on her big, two-story farmhouse and dead branches over

the roof; walkways and steps getting slowly
swallowed up by the earth; ivy climbing up one
side of her house and chimney; shrubs growing
in front of the first story windows; grass growing
too tall; leaves drifting into their own piles; fallen
tree branches and twigs littering the yard. The
property is beyond well established and on its
way to ruins.

Alexine's old eyes smile as she follows his tour
of her beautiful ruins. The winter was especially
long and brutal. Its howling winds were so
frightful, its days and nights so long and dark
and colorless, that it began to seem permanent.
People can forget the miracle of spring until it
really and truly arrives. Then, it's a race to catch
up.

"What can I do for you, Earl?"

"Well now, Alexine, I can see you've got your
hands full. I just wanted to stop in, say hello and
all. Been too long," he says.

Alexine leans on the rake, resting both hands
on top of it. She looks at Earl as if seeing him for
the first time in a long time. "Gee, thanks Earl. I
appreciate that. It's good to see you. How're your
folks?"

"They're managing. Spend all their time
wiping up after John."

"I can imagine. Leaves you to fend for
yourself, huh?"

"Nothing new there."

"I know," Alexine says and looks at where his eyes would be, behind his sunglasses. Instead, she sees a dark, warped mirror image of herself. She turns away and resumes raking.

"Ever think of selling this place and doing something else, ya know, maybe go down to Florida?"

"Florida?" Alexine chuckles.

"Or the Carolinas? Or Arizona, or even California."

"I am this place. I couldn't pick up and go live somewhere else even if I wanted to, which I don't."

"What're ya gonna do, try and keep this place up til the day you die?"

"Yes," Alexine says. "That's exactly what I'm going to do."

"Come on, this place already got the best of you. Look around!" Earl waves his arm around the property like the hand of a clock.

Alexine sniffs and makes a short speech: "Well, that's the way it goes. But the thing about this land is that the ground stays put, doesn't go anywhere. We take care of each other, the land and I. All natural and makes sense. I like that. When I go, I'll leave something of actual value, not more concrete and steel bridges to nowhere. I know where you're going with this, Earl, and I'm not taking the ride today. Uh-uh."

"Okay, well," Earl says, putting up his hands. "More to life than things that don't move. And who the heck are you leaving it all to? In case you haven't noticed, you're the last one of your people left."

"Thanks, Earl, I appreciate that," Alexine says and keeps on raking.

"I know, I've heard, you're dead set against this whole highway extension and bridge idea they're putting out there now, but it could be the ideal time for us to make some big moves."

"Over my dead body."

"Come on, now. Why be like that? You know, you're really making quite a fuss. I've heard about your calling and writing and all, trying to kill the deal before it's even hatched. Some people don't like that, ya know."

"Some people? People like you, ya mean?"

"Come on, Alexine, your farm ain't all that big anymore, but what it's lacking in size you're making up for in breath. Why not hear what some of us have to say?"

"I've heard it all before, Earl. You're a lot younger than me. It wouldn't hurt for people like you to listen to what people like me have to say. Put a highway and a bridge like that up, and you can say goodbye to a whole way of life, a way of life which by the way, feeds people. Don't get blinded by the prospect of big money, Earl. Think about what you're doing!"

"I'd love to say goodbye to all this," he says.

Disgusted, she rakes away a patch of leaves, exposing raw dirt and tender grass. You and I inhale deeply. "Let me guess, the good old boys sent you around, thinking you might talk some sense into me?"

"You never know, you could change your mind," he says.

"Not likely."

"Alright, well, I'm gonna take off, but you think about it," Earl says, heading back to his truck. "By the way, new people moving into my rental cottage Memorial weekend. From the city, with two kids. He's going to work for the newspaper. He's a reporter." His voice oozes with derision when he says the word "reporter" and nods up the wooded hill between her property and his rental cottage.

"Right," Alexine says and salutes Earl casually. "You take care of yourself."

Prompted by the sheer weight of my satchel, I check inside. What I pull out is a special dispatch in triplicate with the title "DISCONTINUED" with Alexine's name and date of birth. I'm to deliver the pink copy to her.

You say we can't just "discontinue" Alexine like that.

I agree to put it back in my satchel and carry it for now.

Earl gets up in his truck, starts it, and roars down the driveway in a new cloud of disruption.

Alexine resumes raking the heavenly scented earth.

We stay to observe.

Chapter 10: A Charming Foe

Wow, isn't Earl lovely. I'm being sarcastic.

And what about Alexine. Sounds like she's a solid no on the bridge. She's on a crusade!

This is a setback. How in the world are we ever going to complete our reconnaissance mission and get back to base in light of this bridge controversy? It's forcing us to take a slow, scenic route down Sumditch Avenue.

It has been rather scenic. This beautiful place

with its sea and sky and land is enchanting. But we're not on vacation. We've got to focus.

Waves of a very fine and very rare scent reach our nostrils in that moment. Leafy, grassy spring dirt entices us to take deep breaths, and the closer we get to the long claws of Alexine's rake, the more concentrated it gets. Soon, we're both giddy again.

We struggle to maintain the clarity achieved only moments ago. Instead, we're dirt connoisseurs now, comparing the terroires of Sumditch Avenue. This is by far the sweetest.

Alexine's hands grip the rake handle again, and she pulls more leaves onto the tarp. She pushes wheelbarrow loads full of twigs and larger branches to the barn to be sorted, cut up, and used as kindling.

Finally, she puts all the gardening tools away and wanders with the dog out front again. Like us, she inhales deeply and looks at the yard's sunny green transformation. She pulls a few choice clumps of greens still clinging to dirt and walks them inside the house.

She puts her early spring bundle into a glass jar and removes her muck boots and jacket. Shoes, boots, and supplies line the mud room floor. Bunches of dried herbs hang from the walls and ceiling.

She takes the fragrant jar upstairs to her

bedroom nightstand and comes back down to the kitchen. She makes honey and cheese sandwiches and eats them hungrily over the sink, looking out the window. Boy, when you're hungry like we are, everything looks delicious.

She freshens water bowls for the dog and cat. A whistle blows on the kettle, and she makes a strong cup of tea.

We are absolutely delighted by the inhaled steam, which leaves little droplets on the end of our noses. It's so good for our sinuses and complexions. We must say, this mission feels at times like a spa, it really does.

After lunch, Alexine's on the go again. This time, it's bees.

With Duke and us on her heels, she goes into a shed past the barn, toward her fields. She takes down from a hook a white veil and places it on her head, pulling the netting below her shirt collar. She puts some pine needles and dried herbs in a smoker, lights it, and steps outside to stacks and stacks of boxes containing beehives.

The bees are taking off and landing, busy at work. After being cooped up all winter, their top priority is a good spring cleaning. Alexine inspects the colony for mites and disease, checks on the queen bees, cleans up around the boxes, and clears space to prepare for a new season in the life of bees. Her movements are practiced and methodical.

Bees pollinate crops, but also this many hives must produce a lot of extra wax and honey. I'll bet she makes lots of products that last forever. We can see that she is devoted.

Incidentally, I note that in spite of their huge production value, the bees don't cause any buzz of points in my wallet.

When she's done, Alexine takes off her veil and puts away the beekeeping equipment.

Good heavens, she's off again!

We all follow her down to her farm stand at the end of her driveway, next to the road. She brushes off the counters. From a container of large black letters, she spells out "OPEN SAT" twice and affixes them to both sides of a sign that can be read by motorists from either direction.

She props the sign up next to the road just as a sporty green convertible zooms down the hill. It's a spectacle that comes with a lot of points!

The car's going too fast and veers into the double yellow lines on the turn. There are two men in the car, with the taller one sitting in the passenger seat gripping the dashboard. They whiz past so fast our heads spin! But we know who they are. One is driving, and Steve is holding on for dear life!

"Idiots," Alexine mumbles to herself, watching.

In a moment, she goes back inside the farm stand, takes out a pad and pencil from a drawer, and she writes a list: asparagus, spinach, early flowers, herbs, honey, salves, candles, soaps. From her pocket she unfolds and reviews another list: OPEN flag, cash box, price list. She locates each of those things and puts check marks next to each.

Now, Alexine goes and stands beside the road again, staring out, lost in thought. Duke wanders over and stands beside her. It's so quiet. Not a vehicle on the road now.

There's a buzzing sound, we all hear it. The buzzing gets louder. It's One and Steve again! The two idiots career by, this time going the other way. Their headlights are on now, and the windshield wipers, too, even though it isn't night or raining. One has two hands on the wheel, and Steve fiddles with the switches while holding on for dear life.

Alexine pulls the dog several steps back to safety. She has fire and damnation in her eyes when she raises her fist and and curses them. She's really mad! Wow, she can be quite fierce, boy oh boy.

A disgusted Alexine huffs and pivots, her feet sending up circular swirls, to walk up her driveway.

We follow her, anticipating a nice quiet

evening in the country, a little time to rest, maybe cuddle up to a fire beside furry animals, and perhaps have something to eat. Like an old fashioned visit with a country cottage grandma!

Besides, we'd be remiss if we didn't conduct at least casual surveillance on our local anti-bridge activist.

Really?

Yes, really.

Our unwitting hostess calls it a day and goes inside. She heats up the world's best soup and brings it into the living room, which is well lived-in considering it's only her and the dog and the cat — pet hair, fireplace ash, empty glasses and dishes, half empty and completely empty bottles, pillows of various colors and shapes, blankets, books, records, papers, and clutter on every surface of the living room, including the floor. Clearly, she has asked herself countless times whether a task is truly necessary and decided not.

Eventually, she sets a fire in the fireplace, and we curl up in front of it next to Alexine's pets. Warmth radiates through us and off our skin to join warm air currents rising and circulating back down and around.

It's so cozy. This is everything we could have asked for, after all we've been through!

In the evening, she repeats into the phone the same story of Earl's visit to multiple people.

She runs down the same three action items so many times in such a calm tone that it becomes a chant: call a friend, write letters, go to public hearing.

Wow is she good.

Eventually, we're lulled into a deep sleep with one question on our minds: if we couldn't ever leave, would that be so bad?

Later, in the wee hours of dawn, Alexine wakes up on the couch. The fire's out, and we're all creaky and cold. She shuts off the lamps and climbs the stairs. Her dog, cat, and we interlopers follow close at her heels.

In her bedroom, she slips off her slippers and gets under the covers fully dressed. She leans over and takes a few deep breaths from the jar of spring greenery and dirt on the nightstand.

Just delicious! Big breaths of yellows and golds, of sunshine, verdant dandelions, sweet dirt and honey swirl in our noses.

The woman's sheets smell like summer herbs and flowers. The soft bedding is like sleeping on a cloud.

We all settle in for what is left of the night.

But now that she's awake, Alexine is restless.

She tosses and turns.

If I may say, she's keeping us awake!

Alexine pulls back the covers and sits up. She puts her slippers back on, and a dressing gown, and is down the stairs before we know what's happening.

We're on the move!

Chapter 11: The Wooded Path

We try to keep up with Alexine. She's already at the back door. She switched into her mud boots, jacket and hat. She's filling a basket with homemade bread, jam, honey, and a card with pressed flowers encased in waxed paper. Then she adds little things from the mud room: a small compass, a small spool of twine, a tiny magnifying glass, a small sewing kit, quarters, hard candies, pieces of chalk, small pocket notebooks, and a whistle.

We get a small infusion of points. The sensation is faint for each object, but as a collection, it's enough to indicate significance.

We all go out the door and head up a path into the wooded hill. Duke is out front.

The path is barely visible in the dawn's earliest light, but the old woman knows the way. Alexine stops every so often along the path, placing small objects from her basket at the foot of certain trees. She pins ribbons waist high on the trees with prizes.

The sun is coming up behind the trees when we get up to the porch of an empty cottage. A tall, old pine tree grows right in front of the porch. Alexine leaves the basket and its remaining contents: the bread, the jars, and the card.

We get back to Alexine's farm, and the morning sun is up. There isn't a cloud in the sky.

Inside, she switches on the kitchen radio. You and I instantly get a strong flow of points at the start of the transmission. A deep male voice relays the news. For each headline, we get extra points.

A news announcer says, "In national news, three drunken white men in a car gunned down a black college-bound high school girl. President Nixon expressed the shame and anger of the nation at what he has called 'an appalling, wanton slaying.'"

Then: "Federal drug smuggling charges against Jane Fonda have been dropped, but she still faces assault charges against a local policeman. In response, Fonda said, 'If there was even the slightest belief on the part of the government that I was guilty of any wrongdoing, I would have been indicted.'"

Meanwhile, Alexine leans on the counter over a pad and pencil. She writes "MORE PRIZES" at the top of her paper and underlines it. On another sheet, she updates her list of chores, adding check marks and more items. On a separate page, she writes "FARM ACTIVITIES / CONVERSATION STARTERS FOR KIDS" and underlines that. She goes in her purse and takes out a few singles, laying them on the counter next to her lists.

"The USSR has launched a spacecraft to Mars...." Alexine is now pulling baking ingredients out of the cupboards and fridge: flour, sugar, baking powder, baking soda, salt, honey, eggs, spices, milk, oil, and butter on the counter along with mixing bowls, baking dishes, mixer, sifter, spatulas, and measuring spoons and cups.

"President Nixon addressed West Point graduates. He said he was grateful that the graduating class of 1971 would not see many of its cadets receive orders for Vietnam. Here's what he had to say, 'The challenge to be strong when you want to use your strength for peace -- not war -- this takes a special kind of courage, stamina, and of statesmanship. And I know you have it.'"

Alexine switches off the radio. In the living room, she puts on a record with classical music.

We spend the rest of the morning listening to the magnificent sound of an orchestra, baking and frosting three kinds of cupcakes, and nibbling on leftovers from the fridge. Alexine measures spices by sight in the palm of her hand and sprinkles them into the mixing bowl like pixie dust. Before noon, we're nipping at a bottle of nice sherry.

We make the executive decision to rest in these environs for a little while, you know, to rest up and get ready for whatever comes next.

Chapter 12: A Girl

The dog picks it up first, a rustling at the edge of the woods.

He gets up with a start and moves quickly toward the sound, hair standing on end, nose to the ground, ears pricked, body tense.

From the kitchen window, Alexine spots him crouched, heading into the woods. She stops washing a dish when he disappears. Duke trots back out moments later, tickled as a peach, at what he found: a child.

By the time Alexine gets her most colorful sun hat on her head and her hands dried, the child is gone. No, there! By the chicken coop. Goodness, it's a girl.

In her best sing-song voice, Alexine calls over, "You-hoo! Little girl! Hello there!"

Duke is abashed, in love. His tail is all a-swish with delight as he trots back and forth between Alexine and his girl, until we've all gathered around her.

"Hi," the girl waves and smiles, sweet as could be. She's so petite.

And awfully thin. The recognition hits me like a ton of bricks.

What's wrong, you ask me.

All of a sudden, everything feels heavy. I need to sit down to tell you the truth.

You help me take off my satchel and sit me down right here in the driveway for a minute. It feels good to take that satchel off.

Alexine's big black and white cat slinks over to the girl, and the girl beckons it with her fingertips. She makes sweet kissing sounds. She says, "Hi kitty! Hey kitty-kitty."

"I see you've met Duke, and that's Greta," Alexine says pointing to the cat. Greta rubs her head on the girl's shins. "What a lovely surprise, a young visitor like yourself! Where did you come from?"

"We just moved here from the city," she says and points up the wooded hill.

"Oh! Yes, my friend told me a new family was coming. Well how nice. What is your name?"

"Lily," she says. "Lily Bogle."

"Lovely to meet you," Alexine says, and the girl shakes hands with strength and enthusiasm. So dainty; such fine little hands. So shy and polite. Absolutely beguiling.

"Nice to meet you, too," Lily says.

"I was just going to take a break from my work and have a snack. I have some nice cold iced tea and some homemade cakes. I hope they came out good but I'm not sure," Alexine says. "Do you want to try them with me?"

"Okay," Lily says with a smile, brushing off her hands even though they're quite neat.

"Wonderful! I'll go inside and get them. Be right out! In the meantime, you can keep Duke and Greta company."

Lily's heart is full to overflowing petting her new animal friends.

Look at her rag-a-muffin clothes, her shoes with no socks. Her nose and mouth are small but well defined. Expressive big eyes, pink cheeks.

I get the idea that I may have something in my satchel for her. I dig until I find a dispatch with no title, just a portrait of her. It just came to me, I felt affection. I wanted to give her a gift, something to let her know who she is.

As Alexine comes back out with a tray and a pitcher, I tuck the dispatch into Lily's pocket.

"Here we are, then," Alexine says, setting everything down on the stone wall lining the driveway. The old woman's tray holds two glasses, a plate of small cakes drizzled with honey, and two cloth napkins. The child is magnanimous, willingly co-creating a little tea party, making gestures of sharing and helping, delighting in the pretty little cakes. She is petite, but she is a big girl to so easily befriend an old lady. It is excedingly rare!

Under the shade of her hat, Alexine's gray-blue eyes can hardly take her eyes off of Lily.

Lily nibbles a cake, declares it's delicious, and devours the rest of it. "Mmm, really good," she says when she finishes chewing and swallowing the last bite. The spices in the cake make the child's nose run a little.

"Mmm, yes, not bad," Alexine agrees.

Alexine pours two glasses of iced tea. They drink together thirstily.

"Will you have another cake? I really made too many, and I need help eating them so they don't go to waste."

"Sure!" Lily smiles at the plate of cakes. Alexine puts another cake in the child's open hand. They sit eating and drinking for a while, all of us discreetly watching Lily to the last crumb and the last drop, when the child finally is satiated. She eats like she's quite hungry and always says thank you.

"Lily, that's such a pretty name, like a beautiful flower. Your parents must love you very much. And do you have any brothers or sisters?"

"One brother, Jack. He's fourteen," she says, licking a crumb off of her mouth.

"Oh how nice! You'll have to bring him next time, okay? And how old are you?"

"I'm ten," Lily says, holding out her empty glass and napkin. "Where should I put this?"

"Oh, here, you can put it on the tray, here. Good, thank you."

"You're welcome. Well, I should be getting back," Lily says, clapping any last crumbs from her hands.

"Oh, okay. Well I'm so glad you stopped by. You can come anytime you like and visit me and Duke and Greta and the chickens. You came on the wooded path, right?"

"Yes, and I found little things all along the path!" Lily says, reaching into her pocket to show Alexine. "Every tree that I saw had a ribbon tied to it, I found something underneath."

"My goodness!" Alexine says. "I always thought it was a magical forest."

"Thank you again," Lily says and puts her treasures back in her pockets. She gives Greta, who lays in the sun on the warm stone wall, another stroke. "Bye!"

The fairy-like little thing disappears as suddenly as she appeared.

Alexine sits on the wall watching the child go. She removes the colorful sun hat, and her gray hair falls around her crows feet eyes. She glances down at the tray with empty dishes, glasses and napkins. She gazes back out across the empty yard and driveway, toward the Bogles' cottage up on the other side of the woods.

Chapter 13: The Brother

The next day, two kids come into the clearing from the woods. Lily introduces her brother, Jack, to Alexine's dog, Duke. Boy and dog are quickly at ease. Lily calls attention to the chickens.

Believe it or not, the boy is even thinner than the girl. I'm again overcome with sudden weakness -- stricken I would say. I sit down on the wall.

I pull his portrait out of my satchel to show you a princely young man.

You see the likeness.

As terribly thin as he is, he's also a strong, strapping adolescent male. Just as polite as his sister, he eats hungrily and gulps down all his milk. Alexine gives him more and more until he's had his fill.

He doesn't say much. He's smart, but he keeps his thoughts to himself.

The brother and sister are quite close, it's obvious.

Alexine is spellbound with them both. We all are.

Duke lays nearby, panting, tongue out. A long strand of drool hangs from his long bottom jaw. His eyes and ears follow the group's movement and conversation.

"Do you have any pets?" Alexine asks.

"Not really. I've seen a big orange cat," Lily says. "But it won't come to me."

"Really? Well, you can always visit Duke and Greta here. They seem to like you guys," Alexine says. Duke's ears perk up at the sound of his name. He sees everyone looking at him kindly, and he closes his eyes and pants. "Look at that, he's smiling!"

Of the activities Alexine has on her list, the kids are game for all of them.

Alexine teaches Jack how to use the gas-powered, ride-on lawn mower. He's old enough and big enough, she tells him. He's got a natural ability with machinery.

Lily collects eggs from the hen house ever so gently and sweetly.

The old woman gives them a tour of the whole farm, beginning with the barn and beekeeping shed, out to the fields, down to the farm stand, and back up to the house. Along the way, she gauges their understanding and tests their math. Very good. They listen well when Alexine explains things. They're curious and smart.

Alexine gives them each a small wad of singles for their "work" and thanks them. She invites them both to work for her whenever they have time.

Before they go home, and sensing they're growing tired and hungry, Alexine insists they rest on the grass while she grills up some burgers and hot dogs with all the fixings. It only takes her a few minutes because she has everything prepared. She gives them tall glasses of milk and a plate of honey cakes. They eat their fill.

They leave with a big bundle of fragrant flowers and herbs for their mother.

"Tell your folks I'll stop over soon to say hello, okay?"

"Okay, thank you!" the children say. Jack

leads the way back to the path through the woods, and they soon disappear.

Alexine pats Duke and says, "You like them, don't ya? Huh? Huh? Yeah." She clears up their picnic and heads to the back door. "So polite, right Duke? These kids are different than most kids these days, who are brats, let's face it. No manners whatsoever without being prodded."

Darn, I didn't give Jack his dispatch. The dispatches must be delivered. These portraits clearly need to get to these children as part of our mission. It's not what I expected, but frankly, we know very little about the mission.

You've gotten through many, many missions before. Your mind is open and flexible, yet disciplined enough to get past the obstacles. I'm glad to be in this trench with you.

My feeling about the Org right now is awe that it can make this happen through its cutting edge quantum technology, but also dismay. I suspect that somehow TS conspired with my ex-therapist, Bob, to send me here.

After the kids disappear, Alexine goes into the house, takes off her mud boots and hat, and collapses on the couch in the living room. There, she goes over lists.

We let Alexine do her own thing, and we follow the children home to deliver the dispatch to Jack.

Part of me resists going up there, to be honest, but there's no choice. The children's almost magical appearance at Alexine's, the visceral reaction I got seeing them, and their portraits on dispatches tells me beyond a shadow of a doubt that they're significant in our Outer Lands mission.

Here's a thought: if something happens, and you and I get separated, how will we find each other?

We agree that if we lose each other, we'll meet on the same beachhead where we came ashore. Near the Dead End sign.

Chapter 14: City Folk

You and I catch up with the Bogle children on their way back home. Lily rides on Jack's back, and he carries her easily along the wooded path.

At the Bogle cottage, the tall pine next to the porch is swaying in the wind.

A woman sits on a chair in front of an easel in the front yard. In contrast with the children, she is quite plump. She is dressed like a gypsy with colorful skirt and dark eyeliner.

It's really a perfect afternoon! Sunny, breezy,

and this woman doesn't have a care in the world.
She dips a brush like a wand into a gob of paint
on a pallette, draws a careful line, and makes a
few dabs. She makes little flourishes with her
wrist.

Now she lights a cigarette and stares at what
she's painted like she's looking in a mirror.

Jack goes in the house, and Lily goes to the
woman. The woman flicks her brush around in
a carafe of muddy water, her arm a gate past
which the child cannot pass. Lily adjusts herself
to stand beside her. Holding Alexine's bouquet,
she says, "Guess what, Mama, this nice old lady
through those woods, she has a farm, and…"

"Shhh! Not now, I'm in the middle of putting
in some final touches," the mother says.

"Oh sorry!" says Lily, exclaiming at her
mother's painting. "That is amazing!"

"Honey, my throat is so dry, would you go
inside and get me a nice big glass of water?"

"OK, Mama!"

After this small errand, Lily sits quietly on the
porch and waits for her mother to finish painting.
You and I sit beside her for a little while watching
the wildlife: a robin hopping along, a pair of
cardinals whizzing by just overhead, a rabbit
grazing, a squirrel. The child gazes out in a dream
state.

She wanders over to the old tall pine tree and lifts herself onto the lowest limb. Then she climbs up, up, up, one branch after another, getting smaller and smaller.

We go up, and before long, we reach the tippy top. Wow, what a view! We're high over the field, and we can see little pieces of the neighbors' properties off in the distance: Alexine's farmhouse down the hill and the Dempseys across Sumditch Avenue.

Lily is fine until a gust of wind hits the top branches and the whole tree sways. Luckily, the little thing has a tight hold on those top branches. She closes her eyes and screams in such a high frequency that only angels would hear.

No one answers.

The gust stops, and she gets ahold of herself faster than you'd think possible. It's a well-toned muscle of hers, we can see that. Blindly, slowly, she descends, screaming involuntarily whenever the wind gusts.

Finally, she reaches the bottom. She sees Jack coming out the front door and runs to him sobbing so hard that she can't speak. He holds her.

"Didn't you hear Lily screaming?" Jack demands, staring wildly at their mother. That is my cue to take his dispatch and put it in his shirt pocket. I pat it to make sure it stays there near his heart.

"What is it now, Jack? She's fine! She just has to be the center of attention!" the woman says. "If you heard her screaming, why didn't you go running?"

A vehicle pulls up the driveway. A man gets out and goes right over to the mother. He gives her pouting mouth a kiss. She complains that the kids are driving her crazy. "Here we have all of this open space now, and all they do is act like helpless babies. Am I or am I not doing something? Does it matter to anyone?"

The father listens, and the way that he looks at the children, he's about ready to take them both on a long walk through the woods and leave them there.

It's easy to see why fairytales are so classic. I make a note to look up the archetypes and pathos of ones that resonate most with me.

When the father walks to the house, he walks straight ahead, clearly irritated. He says, "Lily, you've been up to your antics again, knock it off! And Jack, watch how you talk to your mother."

The father is very angry! He slows his pace down a little near Jack. We see Jack flinch and Lily about to fly to his rescue. But the father keeps walking straight into the house and slams the door behind him.

Our gaze goes from the crestfallen children

to the landscape artist. You rummage around in your satchel, take out a wad of dispatches, walk over to the easel, and wipe the pages all around and into the wet paint. Inspired by your swift and just act, I add a dispatch from my own satchel titled, "ART?"

Although the effect isn't visible to anyone else, the mother does somehow look suddenly dissatisfied with her masterpiece. She theatrically throws her brush down. She, too, walks past the children and into the house, mumbling.

As the sun sets, a light goes on in an upstairs window. Like moths, we're drawn to the bare lightbulb. We receive a few points each.

We watch the man feed paper onto the roll of the typewriter and hunt and peck for letters on its keyboard. He sits and thinks for long periods of time. He takes large bites of the sandwich he brought up. When the sandwich is gone and the beer can is empty, he nibbles on his fingers. When those bleed, he scratches his balding head.

I have to shake my head. Wow, from where I'm standing, these parents are a pair to beat a full house.

Oh look, he's typing something.

What does it say?

It says, "CONTROVERSY AHEAD OF BRIDGE HEARING by Dylan Bogle."

That gets our attention!

An eternity passes, and he types more, pausing periodically to pull the lever across the page. The typewriter makes such a nice dinging ring! Points flow to us with every line.

Well, I must say, Dylan Bogle wasted no time latching onto the biggest story in town and speaking to everyone along Sumditch Avenue, the proposed route to the new bridge. The public hearing is coming up soon. We make a note to be there.

But let's get out of here for a while. Jack has his dispatch, and Lily has hers. You delivered a few of your own for good measure.

As for the Bogle family's stake in the bridge, officially they have none. They're only tenants of Earl Butts, and he's all in.

It's Alexine who is dead set against it.

Chapter 15: Accelerant

We go back to Alexine's and find her down at the farm stand on a mission of her own. She's filling a large carton: daffodil bouquets, three small dried herb sachets, a jar of raw honey, a jar of fruit preserves, bunches of spinach and asparagus, and a tin box of homemade cakes.

She loads the carton into the back of her truck, and we stand there reveling in the country bounty. What a treasure trove! We pick up a

mixture of sensory timestamps of this glorious
new season and seasons that came before.
Alexine's devotion to her farm, her animals, and
the natural world are evident here, all gathered
into one box. It's powerful to our senses and
wondrous to behold. It's medicinal, delicious,
and enchanting.

Look at her prices. They're quite earthly and
don't nearly account for the magical content
of her products. In a way, she's more of a farm
apostle than a businesswoman.

Checking my wallet, I note that the value
of this wonderous collection doesn't register
in the Org's accounting on this mission. It just
doesn't count, garnering no points. Our visit to
the Bogles, however, seems to have really tapped
us out. We'll have to be on the lookout for the
machinery and such that earn points.

Alexine drives this bounty across Sumditch
Avenue and up a dirt driveway to a small cottage
on the Dempsey farm. She gets out, carries the
carton to the door, and knocks.

A woman answers the door, and behind her
stand two girls. The younger girl cowers behind
the older girl, who stands behind her mother.

"Hello," the flustered woman says, smiling
politely, tying her bathrobe.

"Hello, I'm Alexine, I live across the street.
That's my farm there. I just wanted to welcome

you to the neighborhood with a few goodies."

"Oh, hi! Nice to meet you! Thank you so much! I'm Florence, but call me Flo, and this is Veronica and Darla." Flo touches each of the girls' heads. "Say hello girls."

The girls say hello with small hand waves and shy smiles.

"Hello girls," Alexine says to them. "Such enchanting girls."

"Thank you," Florence says. "Girls, say thank you."

Alexine beams at them, "Have you met the Bogle children yet, Jack and Lily, from up the road? They're about your age. They just moved in recently, too."

They shake their pretty manes. Veronica is about Jack's age, and Darla is about Lily's. Perfect.

"Well, I'm sure you'll be going to school together in September, but in the meantime, it just so happens they'll be at my farm on Saturday. Why don't you stop by and meet them?"

Alexine is trying to arrange for all the children to make friends. Remarkable.

When Jack and Lily arrive on Saturday, Alexine doesn't mention her invitation to the sisters, but she has an extra large supply on hand of iced tea and milk, cakes, cold cuts, and bread. She's ready with lists of entertaining activities and topics of conversation for children in case they need prompting. Kids often struggle to make conversation, lacking the courage and manners to extend the courtesy of interest and attention. Well, the Bogle kids aren't bad, but the sisters will likely need coaxing.

She'll let the Bogle kids help give the farm tour. After a tour and refreshments, according to Alexine's notes, she'll help the girls get back across the road safely. She'll caution all of them about the danger of the road. Sumditch Avenue is like a roller coaster, with no visibility in the best of light, and with unexpected twists and turns. Hold hands and be alert, she'll tell them. Use your eyes and ears. Cross together.

She'll tell them a story about twins who didn't look, didn't listen. One gets hit by a car, and the other has to hold that memory forever. A story doesn't have to be true to make a point.

In the meantime, waiting to see if the girls would show up, Alexine would have the Bogles go about their usual business: take stock at the stand, check the cash box; feed the chickens, cat and dog; mow; weed; cut and bundle flowers. There's plenty to do.

The prospect of having four children at work really is energizing. We all love to watch the children work. They're highly productive and efficient, and they're able to work together as a team. At times, they slow down or get distracted or bored, but Alexine doesn't disturb their flow or micromanage them. The kids always manage to get through their tasks sooner or later, and really, what's the rush?

With help from the children, the old woman has time to tackle things that have been piling up. She seems to have a song in her heart, when for example, she's high up on a ladder, scraping chipped paint from the white trim on the front entry way to the house. She's got pep in her step as she whacks back overgrown shrubbery and fills in driveway ruts. Things are beginning to shape up around the place!

We note that her own work style is quite remarkable, actually. Whereas the children may meander and get lost in their work, Alexine is methodical and effective, practiced and strong. Her breaks are short and deliberate. She regularly interacts with the children, just fills her heart of them, and goes back to work re-energized. She's absolutely relentless.

If only she wouldn't stand in the way of progress. I think about the dispatch I've yet to deliver to her.

The girls do show up, and Alexine immediately launches her planned program. While she's going over her lists, you and I observe the four children.

The Bogle kids, even with the advantage of being there first, are so enthralled with the new girls that they cede the social upper hand immediately. Jack is intrigued, though he plays it cool. Lily, for her part, is desperate for Darla's friendship. Darla knows it and accepts her status as someone to be pursued. Lily follows Darla around, and Darla never strays far from her sister, Veronica. A true maiden, the older sister is quiet and mysterious. Darla often serves as Veronica's interpreter to the others.

"She doesn't like the smell," Darla says. "That's why she doesn't want to collect eggs in the chicken coop."

"She's allergic to dogs," Darla explains.

"She needs to go home soon," Darla whispers to Lily at the table. "It's that time of the month."

Nothing goes according to plan right from the start. Nothing is of much interest to any of them compared to the interest they have in each other. Alexine is dumbfounded at the children's own sophisticated, nonverbal forms of communication. Her conversation starters seem clunky. Bewildered, she serves refreshments and leads the tour herself while they all drag their feet the whole way.

The girls completely ruin the day. And to boot

they leave at the first opportunity. After the girls cross Sumditch Avenue without really listening to Alexine's warnings or story about the twins, Jack and Lily immediately get into a tiff walking up the driveway. It's the first time she's seen them bicker. They persist in it to the point where salvaging the day is hopeless.

"How do parents do it," Alexine wonders aloud, exasperated, after the two leave. She says to Duke, "They're just two ordinary kids after all. The whole generation is a dud."

I could swear that Duke rolls his eyes. He's walking away.

Alexine takes off her colorful sun hat and dusts it off on her pants, suddenly bone tired and fit to be tied. Strands of gray hair fall into her eyes. We file inside, and it's immediately obvious that something has snapped. Alexine is wildly off kilter, and the first thing she does is pour herself a double sherry.

Unassuaged, she has more, and gradually she becomes a tempest: slamming drawers, tossing cutlery into the sink, shoving things around. She mutters.

By the time she settles onto the couch, with Duke and Greta warily nearby, she's the picture of despair.

The atmosphere is draining our energy. Let's get out of here.

I'm a little parched myself. The farm dust is killing me. Has it rained even once since we've been here? Is there a drought or something? I feel pretty heated. Summer heat, no rain, and something is building up on Sumditch Avenue, I can feel it. It's that wave buildup again.

It's fine, everything will be fine, says the veteran Ink Drinker. It's terribly beautiful in this archipelago, cinematic even, and we're making progress. You agree something is building and we'll stay alert. Trust the Org, it wouldn't let anything happen to us, especially on a first mission. First missions are like vacations but with special orders.

That's reassuring, which I needed. The mission is still not entirely clear, and we're going solely on instinct. In any case, I committed to the mission, and that's what I'm going to do.

That's the spirit.

Hey, there's an old bar across from the train station in town. Let's go wet our whistle and sort out what to do next.

Chapter 16: Out For A Drink

Downtown, we slide into the bar on a trapezoid of sunset and neon lights.

We look out at the train station, a simple raised platform. Birds go to and fro. I can't imagine a train plowing through the scene.

Inside the bar, low lights showcase rows of colorful bottles like stained glass. Glasses clink, ice tinkles, and a juke box plays low.

A thin line of smoke rises from a slim cigarette

in the finger tips of a woman we recognize. The mother of Veronica and Darla, Florence, is at the other end of the bar. Her smoke joins a general haze in the room.

A juke box is only an arm's length away. It has its own light and sound system, lines of buttons, and slots for coins. We rake in points just looking at it. We're positively dying to hear some music, any music, even if it's oldies.

We drink it all in as we gather our thoughts on the mission, where things stand and where we're headed.

As the Clerk, I start with the facts. First, in terms of delivering dispatches, we have felt prompted at different points to pull dispatches out of our satchels and leave them with people.

Yes, and the dispatches seem to be targetted and a bit provocative.

I check the points balance in my wallet. We're flush at the moment. Though we've been unable to make contact directly with the Org or with TS, the app seems to be working remotely. After all, it is awarding points.

The mission seems to be on track, loosely speaking. As far as the point system is concerned, you keenly note, as have I, what does and what does not get points in the Org's system. Our sensory perceptions don't get points at all! Yet you find them to be most rewarding.

As do I! And what am I going to do with the points, anyway? As far as I can tell, they're non-fungible and only valid with the Org. And yet, there's something so reassuring about them!

You note that on top of the mission, there's the added problem of getting off the island back to base. We're definitely following those leads to the bridge. In a way, it seems central to the mission.

I couldn't have said it better myself. Speaking of which, a public hearing is coming up about the bridge. We cannot miss that.

We do a a quick run-down of stakeholders in the bridge. Alexine wants to sink it. Earl is all in. What about the Dempseys? It's hard to tell where they will weigh in. They might want to keep things going on the farm as they are, or they might want to do something completely different.

I point at the door. There's Earl. Look at him, he thinks he owns the place. It's getting dark outside.

Earl walks right back to Florence, and the two get acquainted. Casually, Earl places his hand on the bar. Now his arm blocks anyone else's access to her.

She's pretty, but no spring chicken.

That flouncy dress of hers is quite becoming.

Three older gents at the bar quietly sip their drinks trying to listen in on the conversation between Earl and Florence.

"Call me Flo," she says.

The bartender cleans a glass with his back turned to the pair, but his ear is cocked, too.

Earl says, "You're new around here."

Florence nods and glances at him. She sips her cocktail.

"What are you having? Let me get ya another."

"Oh this? It's a screwdriver," she says. "Thanks."

"Well, cheers!" They tip their glasses back. "I believe we're neighbors. You're in the Dempsey cottage, right?"

"Yes, that's right."

"You've got two girls?"

"Yes, I have," she says with a smile, delighted he would know that.

Earl notices the old men at the bar staring at them, practically slobbering. He glares at them, and they look away. He turns back to Florence and scans her up and down: shoulder-length blond hair blown back real pretty, cleavage, hips, no wedding ring. "Married?"

"Single, again," she says. She opens a cigarette purse and shakes out a new cigarette and a lighter. Her movements are smooth, practiced.

Earl says, "Here, allow me," and lights her cigarette with her lighter.

She blows a cloud of smoke out into the bar atmosphere.

"Single again? Well, cheers to that," says Earl, and they clink glasses again. A country song starts on the jukebox, and a deep male voice croons and yodels about love.

Soon, Earl is close to Florence, and she arches her back looking up at him.

Looks like Earl may have found himself a willing passenger for his prized truck.

The place is filling up now.

Look who it is!

Kevin Jr holds open the door for the beautiful Francesca, and they walk in. They stop and say hello to everyone they meet on the way to a table. Francesca settles in, and Kevin Jr goes up to the counter and orders drinks toward the back, near Earl and Florence.

Kevin Jr says hello to them, and jovially, he tells her to "watch out for this guy," meaning Earl, which Earl doesn't appreciate.

I mutter under my breath so only you can hear me. "No sense of humor, Earl."

Kevin Jr takes Earl aside and quietly says something to him. Earl sticks out his chin. Kevin Jr pats him on the shoulder, and Earl relaxes.

And here come Earl's new renters, Dylan and Hannah Bogle, the parents of Jack and Lily. They walk right in, right past everyone, and up to the counter. The bartender takes their order and invites them to have a seat at a table.

Kevin Jr goes right up to Dylan and Hannah and invites them to sit with him and Francesca. The two men shake hands. The next thing we know, the four neighbors are sitting together, yucking it up and having a good time. The music is faster, and the din is louder.

At one point, the whole table of four is looking at Earl. They're talking about him, it seems.

A train comes into the station, and more people come into the bar. Folks are keeping the music queued up. We needed this little break from the mission.

I turn to you and say how much I appreciate you. I don't know what I'd do without you, especially with our plane sinking to the bottom of the sea. Here's to us.

To us!

The music slows down to a sultry siren song, and Florence gets ready to go. Her movements have gotten so fluid, she's ignitible. Even Earl looks buzzed when he helps her out of her seat and out of the bar, propping her up by her elbow. Her handbag trails behind her in a loose grip.

We go, too. Outside, Earl closes the passenger side door and walks around to his own side of his truck. As he does, he gets a wild, mean look in his eye. He hocks up a huge wad of phlegm and spits it in our general direction, nearly hitting your shoes. Not for the first time, we are horrified,

disgusted, and shocked at a side of him that's
nothing to write home about.

Soon, the bar empties, and it all goes dark.

Part II: Summer

Chapter 17: Family In Surf

There you are! I wave wildly.

It's nothing short of a miracle that we've been able to rendez-vous at the beach after being thrown into darkness outside the bar in the middle of the night.

We've landed on what can only be described as a perfect summer day at the beach. It's hot, but a breeze blows across the water. Rose-gold clouds parade across the blue sky.

We steal a few moments to soak it all up. Our internal batteries are recharging. It feels good.

What is it about summer, the sun, and the beach that makes us forget everything else?

A beach bag lands in the sand and takes us out of our reverie. A white sheet flutters down to rest under the weight of shoes. A beach umbrella slides open and twirls into the sand.

It's the Bogles, I point out to you.

Oh yeah...

"Go on, leave me in peace," says Hannah to Jack and Lily.

Jack strides down to the water's edge with Lily right behind him.

Soon, who should appear but Francesca Dempsey, who sets herself up next to Hannah's blanket like she does it all the time. Those two really seem to be hitting it off.

"I tried," Francesca says to Hannah as she sips on ice tea and leafs through the latest copy of the National Enquirer. The cover has a big photo of a smiling couple and a top headline about UFOs and anxiety. "I try to be part of his family, but I'm not into the stuff they do."

"Like what?" Hannah says, her face in the sun.

"They're just busy, busy, busy. What are they doing? They're cooking and cleaning, canning and sewing..."

"Um-hmm," Hannah says.

"And juggling calendars! Showers and funerals, christenings and graduations, weddings and reunions. They're always assembling photo albums…"

"And decorating! The wreaths and flags and flowers and candles and…"

"Oh, yes, it's like they keep two sets of calendars. One for the upcoming seasons and one for the actual season," Francesca touches her head, her mind blown. "Because you know those elaborate seasonal things don't just happen. It takes a lot. They take weeks and months if not years of gathering and planning. And then they stand there, all prim and proper, with their hair and makeup perfect, all smiles and good grace, and act like it was nothing at all."

"Like nothing at all," Hannah says.

"And don't forget church and the fire house, and the PTA and the hospital. I'm telling you, these ladies are an auxilliary army!" Francesca says, looking at an article about psychic astrologer Jeane Dixon but not reading it. She closes the Equirer and drops it in her big straw beach bag. "And ya know, they're polite and all, don't get me wrong. But I mean they don't really say much, honestly. It's like one of the rules is to never say or think anything, well not to me at least. And if I do say something, all I get is awkward silence or a blank stare. Ugh! It's so weird. And I get so bored!"

"Yeah? That's not good. Well if none of that stuff interests you, what does? In other words, what would you like to do?"

"Well, I don't know, that's just it," Francesca says, taking a big sip of iced tea. "When I married Kevin, I saw us having a grand life together on the Dempsey's beautiful farm. I don't know exactly what I expected, but as it turns out, I spend a lot of time on my own. Kevin's the only person around here I feel connected to, and he works hard and long hours, especially this time of year."

"I can imagine," Hannah says.

"I've talked to Kevin about it, but what can he do? I need something to do, but I don't know what that is. He says when we have a family, I'll be plenty busy, but I'm not sure that's the answer. I panic just thinking about becoming a mother."

"Well that's the key, finding your own thing," Hannah says. "Why do you think the idea of being a mother panics you?"

"I don't know exactly. It could be because I ruined my mother's life when I was born," Francesca say. "I feel it right down to my bones that my destiny involves fame and fortune, celebrity and romance, not being elbow deep in diapers."

"I wouldn't mind a little fame and fortune... ."

Look who's here! It's Dylan Bogle, just walking toward Hannah's encampment now.

The kids come running up, and Dylan is barely out of his clothes before they grab him for a swim.

Ha! Pretty good, the three of them catch the same little wave together. Jack rides it all the way ashore.

Hannah wades in, splashing her hands and face girlishly. She dives under a breaking wave, her hair flowing backward in the blue green curtain between sea and shore. Her head emerges in the spot where the waves gather to their peaks before breaking. Giddily, she jumps up with the waves without riding them in.

To look ashore from the high point of a wave is a thrill.

When it's time to get out, she uses the energy of the back side of the waves to glide ashore. It's like she's walking on water. Uh oh, she's a little caught off balance in the undertow, and her breasts are popping out of her bathing suit. Dylan is suddenly by her side, and the two act like two teenagers. He takes her elbow to walk her ashore, and she laughs and pushes him away.

Dylan goes back to ride the waves with the kids.

Hannah walks out of the water and up to the

blanket, shaking off droplets. She sits down, then lies down, and doesn't move as she savors the heat of the sun.

Jack's pretty far out, in big surf; Dylan's with him. Uh oh, Lily's trying to get out to them but she's over her head. She wants to go back ashore. She needs help, the little one. Uh-oh, she realizes too late how big that wave got. She freezes, bracing herself for what's coming. The wave grips her little body, whips it around and slams it into shore. She's pinned under roiling white waters.

Lily tumbles and tumbles, held under. She can't breathe, frantic to get a footing in the chaos. Water goes up her nose. She accidentally swallows water. She's really in trouble!

We both break into a run, though what in the world can we do? We're as helpless as she is.

The turbulence abates as we get to her, and the sea releases the poor thing.

She runs to Hannah and wraps her arms around her mother's neck and cries.

"Uck, you're getting me all wet!" Hannah says, pulling Lily off of her. "Here's a towel, just sit yourself down there and get ahold of yourself, please! Now you're getting sand on the blanket! Lily, what is wrong with you?"

Lily sits on the blanket near Hannah and Francesca, who resume their conversation. Lily doesn't interrupt.

You take out a wad of dispatches and pat her little face dry with them and stroke her wet hair.

When the boys finally come back out of the water and stand next to the blanket, they brag about their scrapes with death, their hair sticking out all over.

You can see that Lily adores Jack, looking up at him as he stands there in the sun, his chest glimmering with salt water. Everyone looks at him. Jack has a big destiny, it's obvious. He's the answer to his mother's prayers, the apple of his father's eye, and his sister's best friend. The boy is just magnificent! He's good looking, built lean and strong, at ease with himself, confident. Everyone loves him.

I take a stack of dispatches out of my satchel and glue them individually to Jack until he's wearing a suit of armor. I add a photo dispatch of him to my satchel to remember the moment by.

By and by, you and I go back to sunning ourselves. The air is alive and very special here. We can feel the sandy quartz and tidal waters pulsating, the sun radiating, and our hearts beating.

I ask, where do we go from here?

There's One's estate. Should we see if we can pick up the trail again over there?

We head that way.

Chapter 18: Q2 At One's Estate

We arrive at the estate as One kicks off from the side of a sunny blue tiled pool on an inflatable, oversized yellow duck.

There's a momentary sailing sensation.

Then it's row, row, row; kick, kick, kick. We see all the pretty little water drops splash and fall. Positively good natured is how One feels. He lays his head back on the duck's tail. Sip, sail, soak, sun is a winning formula for an afternoon.

After circumnavigating the pool, he wants to get out. At the ladder, Steve is there waiting with a plush towel and a free hand. He helps One to a deck chair.

Silver rails and puppy dog tails, thank heavens for them. There's something terribly reassuring about standing on terra firma again after bobbing around for awhile. A bracing beverage poolside is the final touch.

Steve seizes the moment to begin ticking off items from his agenda. We can see that Item #3 is "REPORTER RE BRIDGE," but Steve begins with a brief report on One's grown children. Their jet-setting and exploits take a full five minutes according to Steve's beautiful quartz watch.

"Why do they do it?" One is perturbed. "Fly, I mean. My heirs like to fly, fly, fly everywhere," he says, flapping his hands in the air like a bird. "I don't know, given the choice, isn't yachting better?"

Steve is about to reply, but One continues with a salute and a stiff upper lip, "The sea, aye-aye! That's the stuff." One leans back in the lounge chair and puts his face in the sun, then continues, "Wouldn't they like to regale their friends with epic tales of the sea and exotic ports, be part of man's great seafaring tradition? See the world by sea, out on the virgin ocean, with the great deep below and no land in sight, far away from all the busybodies.”

“It’s quite alluring, Sir.” Steve says.

“Yachting’s a slower pace, the jet set is too antsy,” One says and takes a few large gulps from a large frosty glass containing a clear beverage and tinkling ice cubes.

It’s a hot day, and the pool and the ice cubes are absolutely delicious.

“Ack! Something’s wrong with that generation. They can’t sit still, can’t concentrate. Frankly, most of them are not too bright. They’ve got no idea what it takes to be the master of your own destiny.”

“It’s worrisome, Sir.”

“I’ve been thinking, as an investor and owner, I’m just like a farmer,” One says, tapping his index finger to the side of his nose. “We decide what to grow and provide ideal conditions. Then it’s Pop! and Poof! Like magic, a little green shoot comes up! Whether the seeds are in the ground or in thin air, it’s basically the same thing.”

One swallows the rest of the glass and raises it in the air for a refill. Steve obliges, and One lets his head fall back so his face is in full sun. Drowsily, he says, “It’s time to get me to bed for a short nap before dinner. Send in a couple of young beauties, will ya.”

“Certainly, Sir. I can go over the rest of the

items on the agenda another time," Steve says.

We detect an undetectable amount of frustration in Steve as he closes his agenda and signals for the husky nurse under the pool house awning to come.

"Aw, heck, mind as well bring dinner to my room! I'll ring if I need you," One calls back to Steve, already slurring his words as the nurse escorts him down the path from the pool.

The next day is another sunny one.

One and Steve are poolside again, and Steve is ready with his agenda and a pitcher of his wonderful icy elixir. Item #2 - CONTRACT RENEWAL.

"The crew wants a what? A raise? The gall!" One is irate. Steve takes it in stride, as if expecting it.

"Sir," Steve said, "It's quite an elite group, the backbone of operations here on the island and around the world, and not to mention, they exercise absolute discretion in everything they do, as per the contract."

"The nerve! Tell 'em same contract, zero increase. In fact, I want a decrease and a complete organizational review. Make an example of a few of them, let 'em know exactly where they stand."

Steve puts on his reading glasses and gapes at his notebook. He clears his throat. "Beg your pardon, sir, I believe I misspoke," Steve says, rubbing his brow. "The increase I cited was not concerning the crew. It was concerning the chef's request for imports. He'd like a generous increase in fine, rare, expensive ingredients at the kitchen's disposal. May I agree to that for you?"

"Ha! Quite a mix up!" One chuckles. "Now that makes more sense. Yes! Yes, by all means, give the Chef whatever he needs."

"He'll be delighted, thank you, Sir. The item regarding the crew, ah, yes, now I see it all correctly, their contract is due for renewal. Well, it's quite an extraordinary crew this year, Sir. They said to tell you that they're honored to serve you. They appreciate your generosity and the opportunity. They're only asking for a small increase in order to do a demonstration exercise to thank you. They would make it a crowning day of great satisfaction."

"Well, I should think so. Demonstration exercise?" One says. "Tell me more."

"Hmm," Steve says, scanning the clear blue sky. "A small parade showing off equipment and manpower -- and a gunned salute!"

"I like the sound of that..."

Steve continues. "They also proposed something fun: a dramatic mock fire rescue of a damsel from the north tower; or a mock invasion; or a hunt and outdoor roast."

"Very creative! I'll look forward to it," One
says with drink in hand, striding over to his
yellow duck pool float in the shallow end of the
pool. He kicks off the side and floats toward
the deep end. He sounds enthusiastic, raising
his voice for Steve to hear him. "You know
what would be fun? Here's an idea... the crew's
demonstration parade followed by an invasion of
beautiful naked girls with a paint ball hunt, and,
and, and... a pig roast!"

"I will be delighted to convey your ideas to the
crew, Sir," Steve says. "Thank you, Sir."

One raises his glass to Steve as if to say,
"You're welcome." Then he empties it and raises
it again, tinkling the ice. Steve is Johnny-on-
the-spot with the pitcher. "It's too nice out to be
racking the gray matter," One says looking up,
his neck resting on the duck's tail.

That is Steve's cue to leave One in peace.

One falls asleep, drooling, on the raft in the
sun. A long hook comes in handy for a man
adrift. One startles from a delicious golden
slumber when his ducky is hooked like a trout
and towed to the ladder. A hand up, fresh towel,
a dressing gown, and an escort to a shaded
lounge chair -- Steve to the rescue!

One waves away Steve's agenda. Looks like
it's early to bed and so forth again. "That's what's
needed," One says.

The nurse in uniform reappears to escort the man to his bedroom.

You and I are both shaking our heads.

The next day is dreadfully hot, so hot in fact, that One prefers the inner depths of the cool stone walls. At a reasonable hour, he and Steve go to the lower level where we find a hub of subterranean activity. One gazes at all the little red and green lights.

What the dickens do they mean?

Well it's all data.

The blinking lights fill our pockets.

"Data, data, data," One says, as if hearing our question. "What are we seeing today. Look at it! Like a great stream it flows, it finds obstacles, it shows pathways. It radiates outward in a big beautiful halo. Ever wise and efficient, it monitors and corrects itself. Just glorious to behold. The whole thing sets in motion with the tiniest spark."

A man stands at the boards ready to report. This is no doubt another brilliant assistant practiced at the art of patience to make his presentation. The man says, "The dollar is buckling under inflation, so Nixon's pulling the chord."

"Ha! What balls! God I love him. Now what?" One asks. "Currency is based on whatever we say? What a brave new world, brimming with opportunity. Profit or perish!"

"We're playing around with some ideas," the assistant says. "And we're tracking your Wonderland expedition. We don't have indicators back yet but should have in the near future."

"Good," One says. "Full steam ahead! That's where the real opportunities are, doing what no one else has done before, and before the bureaucrats can stop us."

Watching blinking reds turn solid green dilates One's pupils. An auction-like frenzy and willing buyers are such a rush. The operation is like a powerful drug racing through his veins straight to his pants. He grins.

Steve ushers One over to a quick presentation of the plan for the new bridge, including a poster-size notice of public hearing. Kudos to Steve for making a colorful presentation to help One get through the torment of work. The truth is, work is necessary or things slide into chaos that compounds like interest.

"I really am impatient with this bridge project," One says.

"I understand, Sir, and as you can see, it's progressing. There's a local reporter who wants to interview you about it," Steve says.

I wonder who the reporter is, and you bet it's none other than Dylan Bogle.

"Wants to talk to me?" One says. "I'm only the guiding force, I'm not an engineer. What does he want? I don't give interviews, you know that."

"Yes, no, I know, Sir, but the reporter's quite relentless in light of the upcoming public hearing."

"Hearing?"

"Yes, the Tuesday after Labor Day, at Town Hall, he's doing the full story and heard the impetus for the bridge is coming from you. It could be a chance to promote the upsides."

"Heard from whom?"

"Well, he was bound to hear about you from somewhere," Steve says.

"Fine, but only a brief interview. I'm sure I can make the case for the bridge to a low-level town reporter," One chews on his lip. "And it will have to be here, I'm certainly not going to meet him down there."

"I'll arrange it, Sir."

"Here's an idea. Why not time the interview with the demonstration parade the crew's putting on here, shame to waste the spectacle. Just make sure he's gone by the time the fun really begins." One winks and starts for the door. He seems to be done for the day. "That's it, Steve, good, put that together, that could really be a good show, great to have some media here. Frankly, I've earned it. Look how hard I've worked! Look around! One doesn't get here doing nothing all day."

Steve says, "I will take care of it, Sir."

One says, "Make sure it all goes off without a hitch though. You don't always have a firm handle on reporters who are determined to put everything I say or do in the worst possible light."

"Understood, Sir."

"Good." The strain of accomplishing some work deserves a treat. "Now I'm quite done with work for the week. Let me have one of my little blue pills, there's a pretty little thing with my name on her."

"As you wish, Sir," Steve says and fishes in his jacket pocket for a prescription bottle. "Here you are, sir, but remember the doctor's warnings. Your heart..."

"Yes, yes, yes, thank you, Steve," One says, flapping his hand toward the bottle to hurry the man up. "That will be all."

"Very good, Sir."

As we ascend the stairs into the light, I note the post Labor Day public hearing on our calendar.

God, what an ass One is. However, as you rightly note, he's got something we need: the bridge. You take one of your dispatches from your satchel and pin it to his back.

One stumbles going up a step, as these guys

do, and Steve is there to steady him. One takes hold of the rail.

I give you a look of surprise mixed with amusement.

Reaching the top, we assess that we may as well go back to Sumditch Avenue to deliver more of these dispatches. I don't know about you, but my load is feeling lighter every day and not just because of the dispatches drying and getting delivered. I'm sure it has something to do with your camaraderie.

You thank me for saying so, and you feel that the mission may yet get completed. Progress is being made. While we wait for the bridge to materialize, we may as well head back to Sumditch Avenue. We seem to be delivering quite a few dispatches there, and it is beautiful on the farms and the beach.

Chapter 19: What Artists Do All Day

Back on Sumditch Avenue, we look for the kids.

They aren't home. As it's summertime, school's out, and they could be anywhere.

Only Hannah is home, and she appears to be doing nothing at all. It's hard to tell with artists since most of their work is all in their heads. Look, there's smoke coming out of her head now.

She's smoking a cigarette.

Hannah sits near the easel smoking, sipping coffee, and flipping through an art book for inspiration — Rembrandt, DaVinci, Caravaggio, Renoir, Van Gogh, Picasso, Goya, Kandinsky, Matisse, Chagall, Hopper, Pollack, Warhol. Juggling everything, the book slides off her lap and onto the floor. To retrieve it, she puts her cigarette on the ashtray. A few drops of coffee fall from her mug onto the book still on the floor. "Dammit!" she says. She puts her drippy coffee mug down on a pile of newspapers.

We have to shake our heads.

Look at this newspaper cover article. That's old Alexine on the cover, of all people. She's carrying a sign that says, "THE END IS NEAR!" It's Dylan Bogle's name on the article and the photo credit, too. The photo caption says: "A weekly riot of color, chanting, and signage led by local farmer Alexine Wells parades in front of Town Hall to protest the proposed bridge ahead of public hearing."

Wow, you say, she is really, really against this bridge! Look at her, look at that sign.

She really is. But good for him, Dylan Bogle, cover story already! First rate reporter, he must be. Already assigned to one of the biggest stories around town. I can feel his strong, guiding belief in the sanctity of journalism.

The article is titled "REGULAR RIOT AT TOWN HALL," all in big caps like that.

The article begins, "Protesters claim the project is a back room deal that would herald the end of the world as we know it.

"The highway extension would be a knife through the heart of a way of life that's seen us through from the beginning of time, farming, and they want to replace it with development that only benefits the rich,' said Sumditch Avenue farmer and resident, Alexine Wells, the apparent leader of the growing and boisterous gathering. 'It's a bridge too far. Without farms, there's no food!'

The plan as outlined by planners calls for Sumditch Avenue to become a highway. It would take vehicles to the end of the island where there would be a new bridge to the mainland. The bridge would increase traffic as the route becomes a scenic and commercial thoroughfare.

'What kind of diabolical alliance of interests would come together and make that sound like a good thing?' said Wells. 'The only industries we'd have left would be tourism and real estate. Farmland that doesn't get paved over will become nothing more than a subsidized museum.'

The town supervisor said he wouldn't comment until after the public hearings so as to give everyone a chance to be heard. 'In spite of protests,' he said, 'I have heard from other stakeholders who are in favor of the bridge.'

'It's fine if Alexine and her friends here have no use for the bridge,' said Sumditch Avenue farmer Earl Butts, who heckled the protesters. 'They have no right to tell everyone else what they can and can't do with their property and their life. In this country, there's such a thing as rights.' "

I add the article to my satchel for my report.

Hannah is still doing her balancing act when the phone rings. Now she's super annoyed at having to get up and answer the phone.

"Oh hi Francesca," says Hannah into the receiver. "Now?... But... Okay, I'll be right there."

We cross Sumditch Avenue.

Francesca's a wreck!

Chapter 20: Francesca's Big News

Francesca's in a robe, and she's got mascara under her eyes.

Wow, this place is kind of a mess.

There's definitely a vibe.

We're attracted to a blue-hued light in the living room, so we sidestep Francesca and Hannah and find its source. Sure enough, when we seat ourselves on the soft country floral couch in front of the screen, points buzz into our wallets. We baske in the screen glow.

On the credenza is the neat line of framed photos of Francesca and Kevin, and this time we have more time to look. There's the couple at the beach before they got married, like two movie stars. And there are their wedding photos. They look like royalty.

On the coffee table are piles of tabloid newspapers. I do a double take when I see the bizarre photos and giant headlines: celebrity gossip, the occult, "New Age," aliens, abductions, crimes, and UFO sightings. We sift through quite a few issues.

Hannah and Francesca talk in the kitchen. We smell coffee.

"Yes, I'm pregnant!" Francesca sobs. "I don't want to have a baby! I'm already getting fat! And Kevin's been working all the time, he says there's a drought and things are already not looking good this year. Even Kevin's grandfather's been up on the tractor, and Kevin and his Dad don't like it, but they need him. Kevin's been drinking more and more. He and I fight about money. He says I've gotta ease up on shopping. I asked him if he's thought about cutting back on booze instead. Guess the honeymoon's over!"

Just as she says that, Kevin comes in. Whoa, it's quiet and awkward among the three of them. He greets the women, then goes about his business, washing his hands in the bathroom sink, opening and closing the fridge, making himself a sandwich. The conversation between Francesca and Hannah winds down to goodbyes, and Hannah goes out. Kevin kisses Francesca on the top of her head and leaves, too. Francesca sits alone at the kitchen table, sipping coffee.

We head to Alexine's by way of the Dempsey's rental cottage. We're keeping an eye out for Jack and Lily. Maybe they'll be with Veronica and Darla.

All the kids are down here alright.

Chapter 21: New Gang

It's not just the two sisters and the Bogles but three other boys, possibly brothers. All of the boys are on bicycles doing stunts, with Jack leading the crew by a long shot.

Wow, he's really good.

He really is.

All of them together are a pack already, it's obvious when you watch the group for a minute. As the oldest two, Jack and Veronica head the group.

All of the children are so beautiful, with their fresh eyes and bristling energy. My, how fast they grow in the summer! It must be all the sleep.

The girls sit on the porch steps playing with each other's hair, and occasionally squawk at the boys for getting too close or doing something too stupid.

Earl comes out of the house and eases past the girls down the steps.

"Hi Mr. Butts!" Lily says with her little wave. Darla suppresses a giggle.

"Oh hi, honey," says Earl to Lily. "Aren't you a cute little thing. How old are you?"

"Ten," says Lily, looking up.

"Huh, no kidding, you look like you're like five," he says. "You all behave yourselves today, ya hear?" He walks through the bike stunt pandemonium and gets in his big truck, fires it up, and roars off.

"Jerk," says Veronica, watching the truck go down the driveway. "Don't pay any attention to him."

"He thinks he owns the place," says Darla. "And Mom's totally in love with him, right Veronica?"

"Yep. He stares at us funny though, me and Darla."

"How do you mean 'funny'?" says Lily.

"She means sexual funny," Darla says, emphasizing the word sexual.

"Really?" Lily says, her little nose wrinkled up.

"Butts likes to look at our butts," Darla says, breaking out laughing at the word butts. "He's always touching my sister. She says he even looks at my butt! He's so weird."

"Did you tell your Mom?" Lily says.

"Not yet," says Veronica.

"No, not yet," says Darla. "But he better watch it, because we will, and then it's all over for him."

"Don't tell anyone," says Veronica to Lily. "Swear you won't."

"Promise," says Darla.

"I promise," says Lily.

"Such a waste, a jerk like him having such a nice truck," Veronica says dreamily.

One of the boys suggests a game of tag, and everyone agrees. Jack and Veronica officiate from home base, the porch.

Well would you look at that. Darla doesn't run as fast as she could, I must say.

Meaning what? She wants to get caught?

And kissed, I note.

Lily on the other hand, runs like the wind. Look at her go. The boys really have to run full speed to catch her. She's sporty.

Darla always gets caught and kissed, the boys pinning her down. Lily's the only girl left running free. This goes on for a few rounds, and the pattern is clear as day.

One of the bicycle brothers is pretty fast, though, and he catches Lily but releases her without a kiss. She giggles so hard, it's adorable.

The game runs out of steam, and it's game over. The decision is made for everyone to leave.

"We've gotta go over to Alexine's," says Lily.

"You mean the Hag's?" one of the brothers asks.

"We're going, too," says Darla. "After the chores are done, she's taking us all on a picnic today, over to the cliffs."

"Have fun with that," says another brother. "Hopefully she won't lock you up and eat you."

"Very funny," says Lily. "She's actually not so bad."

"Whatever," says a brother. The boys take off like a pack of crows.

We all cross the perilous road gingerly.

On the way up the driveway, the children undergo a transformation step by step. From boisterous wildlings, they become quiet, quick-stepping children. Lily takes the lead, Jack is right behind her, and the girls tag along.

Chapter 22: Alexine Casts A Spell

Duke greets each one as they approach the house, where Alexine is waiting for them outside at her picnic table. She's got her sun hat on, and she has her lists. The table is piled with food and drink.

"Good morning, children!" says Alexine.

"Good morning," they all say in unison, just as they'd learned to do at school with teachers.

"Please help yourselves. There's cheesy eggs

and bacon, muffins and fresh fruit, juice and milk. Jack and Lily, here are your chores lists, there you go, one for each of you. You girls can tag along and help them until everything's done and it's time to go on our picnic, okay?"

They all agreed. Wow, the kids really plow into this buffet! It is bountiful, and they're ravenous, but they show good manners. They exchange glances when Alexine's not looking.

We detect a conspiracy.

Alexine sips on a large cup of tea and watches the children eat. Duke sits nearby. Greta slinks up and brushes Lily's ankles under the table. Lily looks under the table and pets her, and she invites Darla to do the same. Lily is very focused on Darla, acting as her guide and hostess. Jack passes the bowl of berries to Veronica, who accepts it with thanks. He resumes eating and takes a look at his list from Alexine. What a handsome, self-contained, mature young man.

Alexine says, "We seem to be having a very dry summer, so on top of the usual things, we have to make sure everything is well watered, including ourselves and Duke and Greta, okay?"

"Okay," Jack and Lily say in unison.

"It helps to put certain plants next to certain other plants when you're planting the seeds, right Alexine?" says Lily to Darla and Veronica. "That way the tall ones can give the shorter ones some shade when the sun is hottest. And also, they just help each other to grow strong and keep pests away."

Alexine says, "Yes, very good, Lily!"

Darla and Veronica stare blankly at Lily.

"And when it rains," says Jack, "she collects rainwater and uses it on the plants. Hardly anyone does that."

Here, we can see that Jack has heard Alexine speak — lecture? — about this before. Veronica and Darla turn their blank stares on him. Pleasing Alexine and the sisters at the same time is a tightrope walk for sure.

Veronica is definitely too cool for the principles of agricultural water management. Jack meets her gaze with a shrug and a smile. Her blue eyes light up when she smiles back. Oh dear.

I'm detecting energy between them.

You mean they're attracted to each other?

"In any case, thank heavens for you kids helping out," Alexine says. "I don't know what I'd do without you, especially with everything that's going on in town with this hair-brained bridge idea. I mean, how can they even think of severing our connection to the earth for some other way of life? It would be an absolute travesty if they succeed in building something like that bridge out here, putting a major thoroughfare right through our little town. It would destroy a whole way of life."

"Yeah," Jack says. He and Veronica exchange another one of those looks. In that pretty little halter top, her wavy, dirty blond hair falls on her bird-like bare shoulders.

Alexine notices the beautiful young maiden's got her hardest worker's attention. And Lily is completely focused on Darla, passing the girl biscuits and jam that Alexine made herself from her own stores. Lily, who is ordinarily a very good listener, isn't paying any attention at all to Alexine's bridge lecture.

Alexine calls back the attentions of the Bogle kids, "Jack and Lily, your father is doing a great job of covering the story for the newspaper. People are talking about it, and I daresay that we who oppose it are having an impact. They're not going to succeed in slipping this one past us." She makes a fist and lightly pounds it on the table and raises her voice. "Over my dead body!"

Though partially concealed beneath her sun hat, her face flickers in anger, disgust, and yes, power. I see spittle on the side of her mouth, and her piercing eyes turn on the two lovely vixens, Veronica and then Darla.

I know that look. I get a strong pang of anxiety. It's cutting off my airwaves.

What's wrong, you want to know.

I don't know.

Well, you say, let's both take a deep breath.

Deep breath in, deep breath out.

In, out.

Thank you. That's the Ink Drinker for ya. Calm, wise, compassionate. I feel a little better. I really do, and that breath work stuff doesn't usually work on me.

Good.

"Why destroy this beautiful place," Alexine goes on, "for some unknown future in which this farm doesn't matter? What if the future doesn't work out? If someone's idea of progress turns out to be a disaster? It happens! This is a bridge too far, you can trust me on that."

Poor Alexine. She clings very strongly to her beliefs. I can feel it.

The children eat every last crumb and drink every last drop, and now it's time to work.

"OK you've got your lists, Jack and Lily, but let's all start by clearing away breakfast, what do you say?"

They answer back with half-hearted enthusiasm. They help clear away the buffet, and then they all scatter, away from Alexine's keen eye. Jack goes to mow the lawn, the three girls head to the chicken coop first, and Alexine heads to the beehives.

I think a picnic sounds nice right about now.

Should we just relax around here for the day?

You agree.

She sure is wound up about the bridge, isn't she?

Yeah. Could she actually stop it?

She's a character for sure, and she has a point.

She does. Look at this farm, it's paradise.

It's terribly beautiful but maybe a lost cause considering the forces at work. Change is constant.

Watching the kids work, we see Alexine's plan in bringing them all together. They're energized by each other, and they're flying through their tasks while having fun.

Alexine goes about her own tasks, sprinkling praise liberally onto the children as she goes, and I can almost hear them purr. At this rate, she'll be all caught up and well stocked by winter. She has marshalled the energy of the children to her cause.

The children soon get hungry, and who isn't? Work — well, life! — makes us all hungry. But everyone keeps working well beyond basic hunger and into a more ravenous state.

When they run out of steam and Jack gets a little grouchy, Alexine packs the picnic and everyone takes something to carry as they begin a short hike to the sea cliff. Duke tags along, and Greta slinks behind.

Heat radiates off the dry dirt, and dust mixes with salty sea air to coat the back of our throats as we walk along the farm road. The road is lined with thriving weeds waving in a gentle summer breeze. Honestly, their sweet peppery scent is intoxicating. Birds call and butterflies flutter about dizzily.

Lily finds sweet, juicy raspberries growing wild on the side of the farm road, and she calls Darla over. Soon, we all pause to pick berries off their prickly stems, even Alexine! She takes the opportunity to speak to the children about our natural world generally and the lives of berries and birds specifically, but I'm not listening, are you?

Mmm, delicious!

Veronica pricks her finger and jerks her hand back from the bush and says, "Ouch!" There's one tiny drop of blood on her finger tip.

Jack goes to the rescue, taking a closer look, and applying pressure on her finger with his tee shirt. The group moves on, revitalized by Alexine's renewed promise of a "wonderful picnic" and directed by her walking stick in the direction of the sea.

The sheer scale of the sky is awesome, and large cumulus clouds blow by overhead in triumph.

Duke arrives at a sort of dead end at the sea

cliff and doubles back to shepherd the group, which wastes no time unpacking the picnic and assembling it on a large blanket.

"Gather round, kids," says Alexine. "Let's eat!"

And eat they do. My, my, my, what big appetites they have! There's no talking, just voracious eating and drinking. Sandwiches piled high with meats and cheeses, greens and condiments; peaches; cakes with honey, and thirst-quenching lemonade.

When they have their fill, they ask to go down the cliff to swim in the sea. Alexine agrees, as long as they stay together.

The children scramble down a grassy path and the sandy, bold face of the cliff to the water below. Duke follows.

We move to the edge of the cliff, and the roar of the sea gets louder and louder. Looking out from high up like this is exhilarating!

Alexine walks to the cliff edge and looks first for the children on the beach below, frolicking together in the water, splashing each other and diving around like porpoises, hooting and hollering, having the time of their life. Jack throws Duke a stick of beach wood, and Duke retrieves it and returns it, happy as could be. They all look so happy.

I look back at Alexine and nudge you. You gaze away from the children to watch Alexine, who does something unexpected. With her eyes closed, she raises her arms in the air, jutting her walking stick into the breeze. She takes a deep breath and chants cascades of words as she exhales:

"Hush little wildlings shhh
splashing, shouting in the salty blue sea
sustained by sweet fruits of labor;
may these sacred moraines
cast earthly coordinates
onto your breastbones and
brand your tender flesh;
may you remain innocent
in this sinful world
forever."

Was that... a spell?
You don't know what that was, but it was brimming with spirited belief.
Very strong belief.
Right there on the edge, I jot it down, and I try to upload it to the Org on my device as an urgent dispatch. We wait for a response.
For the love of Pete! What's it going to take to get a response? I'm aggravated.
Back at the picnic blanket, we sit and wait.
Alexine sits there chewing on a grain stalk, thinking. She looks off in one direction, then

looks off in another, then looks at her toes wiggling at the end of her bare feet. She looks in our direction and seems to look right through us.

We lay down, our backs to the good earth, and close our eyes.

My device dings. There's actually a message! It says, "REPORT MISSION PROGRESS; OVER."

What should I say?

Together we compose a response: "CRASH LANDING. PLANE LOST. MISSION IN PROGRESS/BRIDGE PLAN IN PROGRESS. REQUEST ASSISTANCE."

I hit SEND.

It's late afternoon when the kids come back up the cliff. They're exuberant and ready to move on to the next thing.

"What shall we do, kids? Pack up and go back? I can grill burgers before you go home if you like," Alexine says.

The kids love that idea, forgetting their former airs of maturity and restraint, practically jumping for joy. The deep blue sea has restored their childishness. Their camaraderie is very strong now. They all pack up and are soon en route back to the farm.

As well prepared as Alexine is, the kids are famished again by the time everything is ready to eat.

That's when TS buzzes back, "ASSISTANCE

NOT POSSIBLE AT THIS TIME. PROCEED WITH MISSION/BRIDGE PLAN."

I look up to see the kids getting their fill of barbecued burgers and hot dogs, homemade potato fries, tomatoes as sweet as candy, fresh cucumbers, beans, carrots, cakes and cold milk. Not only does Alexine give Jack and Lily money for today's work, she gives some to Veronica and Darla, too.

According to my calculations, the kids could wind up helping Alexine quite a bit. She's got years of projects around the farm to catch up on not including farming tasks -- sanding and painting, minor repairs, cleanup, stocking and storing, organizing and weeding, anyone can see that.

It's not only their labor she's getting, it's her own energy level being fueled. It's quite high.

After all the old woman has done for the kids, her face drops when the kids talk about meeting up and biking to the local summer carnival later.

"I guess it's your money to spend however you wish, but wouldn't you rather save it?" she asks. Alexine looks tired.

The kids stare blankly at her, and then in a flash, they leave to go home.

I have to pocket my device to follow the Bogles up the wooded hill.

When we get up to the cottage, their parents

are in the middle of an intense conversation
about the war and Muhammad Ali.

Jack and Lily banish themselves right to their
rooms to get ready for the carnival.

Chapter 23: Trouble in Paradise

I don't smell anything cooking for dinner.
Apparently there's no dinner in progress.
Good thing Alexine has fed everyone.
The parents turn their conversation to talking
about Dylan's job at the newspaper. His boss and
his "damn red pencil" cross out his best material,
Dylan says. "Any hint of the writer's personhood
must be erased. Nothing funny, no opinions, no
supposing, no stray thoughts, no odd words —

just his old school, by-the-book bullshit! That's his whole job, being the newspaper stiff."

"Forget investigating anything or any real controversy," Hannah chimes in, in support. "Don't reveal how things really are or who's actually involved. Oh no, nothing like that."

"He looks at me like I've got two heads for even thinking about a different angle on a news story. You should've seen how much he took out of my story about Alexine protesting in front of Town Hall about the bridge. He got so mad that he came right out and asked why a reporter who gets assigned a straighforward story would take it upon himself to make things complicated?'"

"Well, I suppose he's not wrong about some of that," Hannah says, playing Devil's advocate now. "I mean, after all, it's a business, it's part of the community. And he is your boss."

"If I get a lead on a big story, if my radar picks something up or I hear so much as a whisper about an interesting angle, I'm gonna hunt it down," Dylan says.

"You're an animal, honey," Hannah says with a laugh.

"He's trying to keep me on a short leash," Dylan says.

"I mean, I don't think you have it in you to do what he's asking. You'd be bored to death," Hannah says.

"We'll probably keep butting heads until one of us can't do it anymore. In the meantime I've got a couple of articles to turn in tomorrow. I'm gonna go upstairs and work on them."

"Okay, and I'll keep working on the series, I've been making good progress," Hannah says with a sigh and gets up. She goes to their bedroom by way of the kitchen, grabbing a snack on her way.

Dylan grabs two bologna sandwiches and his notebook and goes upstairs to work. He pulls the chain of the overhead bulb and shuts the door.

He positions a piece of paper straight behind the drum of the typewriter using its metal guide. He turns the crank to feed it onto the drum and snaps the paper into place.

We get a nice infusion of points.

He eats one of the sandwiches while reading his notes.

In all caps, he types. The metal keys swing up, hit the black ink ribbon, and the ink imprints the crisp white paper. Letters form words, and the words form a headline.

"I'll give that old prick something to do," says Dylan. He pulls a lever across the front of the paper, writes his byline, and then pulls the lever again twice. He unlocks the capital keys and resumes typing. He writes across to the end of the line, and the typewriter makes a delightful bell sound.

Well, those points just pile into our pockets!

He types a whole paragraph, then eats the second sandwich while he rereads what he wrote and checks his notes. He sits and thinks a while. His sandwiches gone, he nibbles on his thumbnail. He rips the paper off of the drum, crumples it up, and throws it on the floor. He puts a new clean sheet in and starts again.

He repeats this process so many times that, with the tapping and dinging and purring in my pocket, I'm overcome with drowsiness. It's been a long day.

I startle when you nudge me.

We note that Dylan's mood has deteriorated. He's hopping mad. He's banging things around, pacing the room, tearing out what little is left of his hair.

We sense something stirring outside of the room. Up until now, it's been quiet in the rest of the house.

It's the kids. The sun is going down. They're leaving the house. They're getting themselves together, counting their money, and going right out the front door without a word to either parent.

Jack puts his bike chain and lock across his chest, and they get on their bikes and take off, with Jack in the lead.

Chapter 24: Veronica Tells

They ride over to Florence's cottage.

The whole gang is there waiting outside by their bicycles for the sisters. The level of anticipation is strong, and we can feel that there's a buzz in the air.

"They said they'd be out in a minute," says one of the neighbor brothers to the Bogles.

You and I drift inside the house. The girls are in with their mother. Florence is in her bed, and

Darla lays next to her, caressing her mother's hair.

Veronica is in the room, picking up dirty dishes from her mother's bedside. She goes out with the dishes and comes back empty-handed with a do-or-die look on her face and tells her mother point blank, "Your boyfriend has eyes for me and Darla, just so you know."

"What?" Florence says and waves it away. "Not this shit again. It didn't go so well for you the last time. Get over yourself, will ya?"

"What, you think I'm imagining it?" Veronica asks.

"You think everyone's in love with you," her mother says, straining to look at Veronica through squinted eyes.

"Oh no, I'm not imagining it. You're so far gone, you can't see it."

"Yeah, right, dream on, honey. Just stick to your little boyfriend, what's his name -- Jack?"

"He's not my boyfriend, he's my friend," Veronica says, getting right in her mother's face. "What about Darla? Are you gonna just lay around, let Earl go after Darla, too?"

"Aw, would you get out of here? Leave me the hell alone!"

Veronica leans in, puts her finger up to within inches of her mother's nose and says, "You! You're a terrible mother. You're pathetic, horrible, weak! You're a sad drug fiend and not to mention uglier and older every day."

Florence slaps Veronica across the face. "You are a fresh, self-centered, little bitch. Now get out of my sight."

Veronica recoils, stunned. "Get rid of him or else," Veronica says.

"Get out!"

"Darla, let's go."

Darla does what Veronica says. They're walking out the back door just as Earl is coming in. He blocks their way with his full grown male figure plus a big brown bag of groceries.

Veronica stops short and glares at him.

He moves out of the way just barely enough for her to squeeze by. "Where's the fire?" he asks her. "And where's you mother?"

"In bed as usual," Veronica says.

As the younger sister passes by behind the older one, Earl does look at their butts.

"Who's supposed to cook dinner, then?" Earl asks.

The girls just keep walking.

He puts the groceries down on a chair and tells the girls to hold up. He catches up to Veronica and pulls her aside.

Earl hisses at lovely Veronica and hurts her wrist. He tells her, "You look like a hooker for Christ's sake."

Veronica's eyes tear up. Her whole demeanor changes to one of defeat and submission.

Jack walks right up and stands next to her.

"Alright?" Jack says, putting his arm around her shoulder. He looks at Earl and asks what's up. Earl is about to answer when Darla and Lily run up to their older siblings. Darla pulls on Veronica, and Lily pulls on Jack.

I ask you, is there anything in the world quite so powerful as little girls?

Jack says, "Come on, let's go," and he guides Veronica toward their bicycles.

We observe that Earl is, in fact, inappropriate with the sisters. It's as bad as Veronica has been saying.

Everyone mounts their bicycles and takes off down the driveway and onto Sumditch Avenue, which we all know is a dangerous road even in broad daylight.

Chapter 25: Love at the Carnival

Jack and the brothers take the lead. Lily and Darla ride behind them, and Veronica pulls up the rear. Cars whiz by.

We're in hot pursuit. We follow this motley crew into town and don't stop until we get to the railroad crossing. Flashing red gates lower to block the road. The bells are clanging! The last train of the evening is coming. The points are electrifying! It's all quite exciting.

The brothers consider going around the gates and beating the train to cross the road. The middle brother peaks down the tracks. He shakes his head and returns to his bike to wait.

We can all hear the train rumbling closer and louder.

Veronica straddles her bicycle next to Jack's. The ground shakes. An enormous old diesel train bursts into the station with a loud whistle. A wall of wind blows through us all. How titillating!

Pushing her hair out of her eyes, Veronica smiles at Jack, who stands there like the knight in shining armor that he is. He smiles back. By the time the train leaves the station, Jack is hopelessly in love.

The train's taillights pass out of the station, the gates go back up, and the kids cross the tracks. The carnival's lights are a beacon in the near distance.

When they get there, finally, thankfully all in one piece, Jack threads his chain through the bikes and locks them to a post.

The rest of the evening is a blur. We're spun round and round on a star ship, hurled down and around on a roller coaster, and sent sky-high on a ferris wheel. Pretty lights of every color in the rainbow sparkle everywhere we look. Sounds of machines, screams, and laughter fill the air. The children run here, then there, and back again.

They fill their bellies with cotton candy, soda, hot dogs and strawberry shortcake. Our wallets are full!

At nightfall, fireworks go off, signaling the start of a long series of powerful explosions and displays of light in the dark sky above. We're transformed by sheer fun and freedom into a cohesive group.

I can feel the strength of its unity.

Yes, it's strong.

When the fireworks show is over, it's time to return home. We know we've been gone too long. It's dark, and we must bike home on Sumditch Avenue.

The next days are as hot and dry as any other, but they're different in that everyone is grounded. The parents managed to notice their children's absence in the night.

It's not long, however, before the parents lose track of the kids again.

Chapter 26: The Rupture

Being peak season, there's plenty of work at Alexine's. She feeds everyone, pays everyone, and then we go hang out together far from view.

Alexine's keen nose picks up on the changes among the kids as of late. She senses the rebellion. A sneer, an eye-roll, a head shake — she wasn't just imagining it. No. Jack and Lily seem different.

After all, Jack's a young man now, and even

Lily is maturing. The shape of her face is getting longer, and her skin is getting acne. Her legs are getting shapely in her shorts, which are getting shorter and shorter thanks to the influence of the sisters.

In the bright sunlight of summer, Alexine can plainly see those special children, who were once enthusiastic to perform farm tasks, now seem to be working just for food and money. They don't ask her questions about farming, about her life, or even ask what's happening with the bridge project.

In fact, watching the kids, it's obvious they're rushing through their chores and not being diligent, and they eat like a swarm of locusts. The equation changes for Alexine, and she loses it.

It begins with a sermon about the importance of hard work in life, about the high stakes of farming with which only fools gamble. She mentions the shortcuts Jack and Lily take lately, revealing the degree of surveillance they've unwittingly been under.

But the worst Alexine has saved for the sisters, Veronica and Darla, "Young ladies, this is a farm, not a fashion show. What you're wearing isn't appropriate. There's no room for any of this nonsense on a farm. If you want to grow up to be loose women, do it on your own time."

Oof! These remarks, which won't soon be

forgotten, land heavily within our gathering. They reveal hostility in the old woman that up until now she has hidden well.

We're all stunned, except for Veronica. She answers right away, "Well, it's obvious that me and Darla aren't exactly welcome here, so we're gonna go, bye."

And they go, just like that, leaving Jack and Lily to face this new reality. They are no match for Alexine. Her age commands respect and compliance, as does her generosity. She puts them in their place, and their powerless position embarrasses them.

Jack and Lily comply by finishing the chores that all of them would have done together, sitting through a quiet meal, and leaving sheepishly.

Watching them, I get a feeling, a strong feeling. Am I struggling a bit with my feelings? It is good of you to notice.

It's that feeling of shame and humiliation. By the time too many children grow up, they've died by a thousand of these cuts.

On the way home through the woods, Lily tells Jack about the situation with Earl Butts and Florence that Veronica and Darla are going through.

For awhile, Jack and Lily both continue going to Alexine's.

Then only Lily goes. Jack spends all of his

time with Veronica.

In the last days of summer before school starts up, approaching Labor Day, even Lily doesn't go.

Instead, the gang gathers in various spaces around the neighborhood: basements, an old broken down jalopy in the woods, the cliffs, and homes in which parents aren't around, for example.

Today we are all here at the Bogle home because both parents happen to be out and where we're relatively assured of no adult interference. We're scavaging scraps and crumbs in the kitchen.

We feel these kids are pure potential. They just need to be fed, protected, and cared for. Alexine certainly does know life force when she sees it.

We just love these kids. I search through my satchel and come up with two dispatches. One is a red card signifying righteous anger, and the other is a red card signifying love. I place them on the kitchen table.

We hear a rumble in the Bogle's driveway. Someone's home.

Good grief, it's a double whammy. Dylan's here, and so is Alexine right behind him. They get out and talk. Alexine hands Dylan a carton of her produce and flowers. We hear a large flock of migrating birds gathering in the trees above, chattering among themselves in a loud din.

Dylan calls out, "Jack? Lily? Jack and Lily!"

Lily goes out on the porch. She waves hello but goes right back inside. The spring on the screen door pulls the wooden frame shut like a rifle shot. The birds in the trees go silent and fly away en mass.

It takes our breath away what a bold move this young lady has made.

That's not how little girls are supposed to behave, some would say.

Dylan scratches his balding head, and Alexine stands looking at the screen door, stunned. It's awkward.

"Hmm," says Dylan.

"Wow, well, I guess I'll be on my way," Alexine says.

"Yep, see you at the hearing," says Dylan. He turns to walk to the house, and Alexine gets back into her truck and drives away.

The bridge hearing!

It's coming up soon, right after Labor Day.

By the time Dylan gets in the house, the kids are gone out the back door.

We catch up to Alexine to see what effect Lily's action has had on her and what she'll do about it.

Chapter 27: Thunder Storm

The sky darkens to the west. A storm is coming, and the air is eerily still as Alexine pulls into her driveway.

Duke meets her truck and trots behind the truck. He's nervous. His ears are down, and he paces around the truck until Alexine gets out.

"Storm coming, aye boy?" Alexine says. "Come on, let's batten down the hatches."

Wind soon rushes in from the west, moving

the treetops back and forth wildly and violently. She takes laundry off the line, makes sure the rain barrels are ready for a deluge, and shuts the western-facing windows throughout the house.

She calls Greta's name but the cat is nowhere in sight. Alexine props the pantry door open a crack so Greta can get back in if she's still outside. She leaves the kitchen window open and stands at the sink watching the storm come in.

Everything is in motion. The first large drops torpedo in, sending ionized rainwater and dust plumes into the air. She inhales the rare but familiar storm fragrance deeply.

We all do.

The Earth's crust is very thirsty, we can feel it. We can feel its thirst, we can feel it getting quenched drop by drop until streams flow down the driveway to Sumditch Avenue.

A flash of lightning electrifies the sky and unleashes a very large beast, judging by the long, low growl outside.

Poor Duke, his courage falters. He sits right on Alexine's feet. Greta slinks inside through the open door and skitters into the kitchen. She runs past Alexine and Duke and disappears into the living room.

The house echoes loud rainfall. Water rushes down the roof, into the gutters and down the spouts. The beast is raining down, the beast lurks in between strikes, the beast lashes out. Alexine grasps hold of a pad and pencil. She finds a fresh page, flipping past all of the lists: the farm supplies lists, the Bogle kids lists, reading lists, ingredients lists, farm stand lists, and stop-the-bridge-project lists.

She stands, pencil ready to write on a clean page.

Surely, without the kids, she faces a new period of loneliness and despair.

Lightning flashes, and strands of Alexine's white hair light up around her wide-eyed face. There is a crack so loud it shakes the house and rattles Alexine's bones. The dog runs under the kitchen table, shivering and cowering, looking up at her for help.

"Shh, it's alright, Duke, shhh, ya big baby," she says. She looks at the large pendulum clock in the living room and jots down the exact time, down to the minute and seconds.

When thunder and lightening strike again, she writes down the exact time again. She's tracking the beast's thunderous footsteps to know when it has arrived and when it's moving on.

Finally, the beast arrives. It creeps into our fingertips and toes. It seizes our bellies, climbs up our spines, and sits on the top of our heads, sharp as pins and needles.

We're terrified.

But we can see that Alexine's powers recharge with every strike of lightening.

Part III: The Fall

Chapter 28: Alexine's Campaign

The surf is deafening today in the Outer Lands Archipelago, where nature speaks powerfully without saying a word.

I find fuselage from our biplane along the shore.

Walls of wild fifty-year waves come steadily. Each one rears up, reaches full height, and crashes.

The tide is coming in, and more sand gets

sucked out from under my feet with each wave.

I'm starting to panic when here you come again, down along Dead End beach, a true hero.

What day is it? Have we missed the bridge hearing? We don't want to miss that.

We hitch a ride to Town Hall and find out the hearing isn't until tomorrow at 09:00. So we head straight back to Sumditch Avenue. There's no time for One's antics.

We get there in time to see a big yellow school bus take our whole gang away.

Bummer.

We find Alexine, the single greatest obstacle to the bridge materializing, at home. She's on the phone.

Her voice comes from deep in her diaphragm. Sound waves go up through her chest, up her throat, over her tongue, through her teeth and thin lips, and into the receiver. Her words go through a curly long wire, to a rotary phone box on the wall and then along wires behind the wall. They go up to the roof and out to Sumditch Avenue, where they then travel via wires strung high up on wooden poles all along Sumditch Avenue and beyond.

That is how, in spite of the distance up the road, Alexine's voice gets to Earl's ear live in real time and with hardly any delay at all.

You and I are loading up on points, that's for

sure! Ding, ding, ding, ding!

"Hiya, Earl."

"Hey."

"Stop over for dinner, I'll grill up a steak for you."

"What, tonight?"

"Yep," she says. "I wanna talk to you about something."

Earl doesn't reply.

"And I've got a big bottle of Chivas I can't seem to get to the bottom of."

Earl clears his throat. "Yeah alright."

"Good, see you at six," she says.

Alexine goes to the grocery store, then the liquor store, then to the gas station, then home. She spends the rest of the day at the hives, in the barn, and at the farm stand. She's gotten dinner started before Earl pulls up, radio blaring country music. A deep-voiced man yodels out a high note, drops down low, and plays a guitar solo.

Right in the middle of the solo, Earl kills the ignition. Suddenly it's dead silent.

Alexine moves large potatoes wrapped in foil to the side of the grill to keep warm and throws the seasoned steaks on the grill. A pot of green beans with butter and salt is on the picnic table along with plates, cutlery, napkins, glasses, butter, salt, pepper, steak sauce, and the bottle of Chivas. From her station at the grill, she says,

"Hey, have a seat! Pour us a drink will ya!"

When the steaks are medium rare, Alexine moves them to the cutting board and brings them to the table. The bees are out in force, attracted by sweet condiments. Male bees are banished from hives at this time of year, never to return. They're full of existential dread and have nothing to lose.

Earl, who is apparently starving, wolfs down his food and washes it down with whiskey. Finally, he sits back long enough to take in his surroundings.

"Hungry, huh?" Alexine says, shaking her head.

Earl belches, "Yeeee-ep!"

"Help yourself, there's more of everything. Don't forget your green beans."

The steaks look delicious and so tender, juices running under the skin of her potato. Alexine eats small bites and chews them well.

Earl snaps his fingers at Duke. "Here, boy."

Duke ignores him.

"Ever notice how," Alexine says, "steak and potatoes go so well together?"

"Sure do. Add whiskey and you've really got something."

While surveying the surroundings, Earl keeps at the dog. Duke continues to ignore him, sometimes looking to Alexine to intervene and tell the ass to stop annoying him. Earl helps himself to more steak.

"How's your brother?" she asks.

"Put it this way," he says. "He's none too thrilled to be alive. Mom and Dad there nursing him night and day. It's killing them all, and that's all it's ever gonna be."

Alexine shakes her head. "Well you never know, miracles do happen, gotta hope. Wish there was a solution to the situation other than the way it is."

"There is, but no one wants to hear about it," he says and lights a cigarette.

Alexine looks up from her plate at him with raised eyebrows.

"Well," he says, "Sell the damn farm, it's worth more for real estate than trying to scratch out a living growing potatoes. Put John in a veterans home. Someplace nice down south maybe. My folks could visit him but not have to wipe his ass."

Alexine makes a noise like she's listening but makes no comment.

Earl continues on to the crux. "I could take Dad fishing and hunting. Get Mom a nice big house and a little peace."

"Ah," Alexine says. "What a lovely vision."

Earl takes a big gulp of whiskey.

"I've got a homemade apple pie, too," she says.

Earl smokes his cigarette to the end and drops the butt on the ground to grind it under his boot. "So you said you wanna talk to me. Let me guess, the bridge hearing tomorrow."

"No," she says.

"No what? No you don't wanna talk about that? Or no you're not selling?"

"No to both. We'll just have to see what happens," Alexine says. "In the meantime, can I interest you in some pie and a refill?"

Alexine carves up one piece of steak for the dog and brings the rest in the house. It's a cool September evening that's quickly going from warm to chilly as the sun goes down.

When she gets back to the table, she proposes they move over to the fire pit for dessert. He gets a fire going while she gets the pie plated.

They have pie, and Alexine throws more wood onto the fire and refills Earl's glass of whiskey. Before long, the fire is raging. They take turns standing there, poking it with a long staff-like stick. Embers shoot and float into the night air. They both stare at the fire quietly for a while. Duke paces around the periphery, sniffing around.

"Well, like I said, there's something I wanted to talk to you about, and it's not the bridge. I wanted to ask you how things are going with you and Florence. I have to say, she seems really out of it when I see her around."

"I swear, the oceans aren't big enough to drown all the gossips around here. Flo just likes to have a good time. Does she go overboard sometimes? Maybe. And that's why I'm always bringing groceries and trying to be there for the girls."

Alexine says, "I'll bet you are."

He sucks in some spit and mutters something about "such pretty young things."

"Well, they're clearly heading in the same direction as their mother if you ask me," Alexine says. "I'm awfully concerned about them. The best thing that could ever happen to them would be to get away from here somehow. I felt I needed to alert you to the situation, and maybe you'd have a solution since you seem to be the man of the house over there these days."

Earl ponders that quietly.

We all do.

Then, in a moment of weakness and inebriation, Alexine describes the sisters' behavior at her farm. She tells Earl about how the sisters even turned the Bogle kids against her. "Those girls are already bad news," she says.

"What do you want with those Bogle kids anyway," Earl says. "Fattening them up for something?" He laughs and laughs.

"Well I took you under my wing when your

parents didn't have much time for you either, as I recall, well before your brother went to war," she says, grabbing the poker and stirring the fire. She jabs angrily at the coals. "Feeding our young and teaching them the value of hard work is what I'm doing. And as for hinting that I'm a child-eating witch or 'The Hag" -- I know people call me that -- that's just the good old boys refusing to admit that it's Mother Nature who holds the cards, not them. It shows them up, my farm doing okay in times like these while theirs wither and wilt under the sun. You all just want to throw down chemicals and sit on your big machines and make as much money as humanly possible, using and abusing the land. When a drought gives you all a reality check, it's obvious how lost you are. You can't wait to cash a big check for this godforsaken bridge to nowhere. It's pathetic."

"Yeah, right, 'the Hag,' patron saint of lost children and farmer of the year. Give me a break," he says, stting back in his seat. "You know, in the good old days, no one would have to listen to a woman like you when it comes to important things like roads and bridges or anything else. We'd just burn you at the stake and be done with it!" He cackles, but now his short hair is sticking up in the back.

More than her comments about a bunch of kids, her challenge to his work and virtue as a man is really making him angry.

They're both getting angry.

Duke walks over to Alexine's side and stands on all fours, staring at Earl. His ears and fur are up.

She says with a menacing chuckle, "You really are hopeless, Earl. People surely will be hearing from me about your dream bridge tomorrow. And not for nothing, but you always were an ungrateful little bastard with a big mouth. Just goes to show you, in spite of what we do, sometimes it doesn't matter, some people are just determined to turn out wrong I guess. Too bad." She throws down the poker, goes in the house with Duke at her heels, and slams the door shut.

"Love you too, y'ole bitch," Earl says and pees on the fire. He stumbles to his truck. The engine roars to a start, backs out, and crosses Sumditch Avenue to Florence's cottage.

It's pitch dark when Earl shuts off his truck, and we walk to the middle of the road and stand there, listening to a low din of night creatures but mostly silence.

We take refuge in Alexine's barn for the night. I love the sweet scent of straw! And dirt. So delicious! We've got the hearing at oh-nine-hundred, so goodnight.

Night.

Chapter 29: Bridge Hearing

This is not what you want to see when you're trying to get a bridge built. It's standing room only.

There is a loud din, and springs squeak as the seats fill at the public hearing for the proposed highway extension and bridge.

Dylan Bogle is up front adjusting his camera and getting his notebook ready, chatting with the attendees behind him.

Alexine is buzzing around the room talking to individuals about what to expect, when to make a statement, and what to say.

She points to the bridge planners up front with the town board, getting ready to make a presentation. After their talk, the floor will be open to public statements. She points to the lectern in the aisle from which they can speak, and she points to open seats.

The three Dempsey men -- Kevin Dempsey Jr, his father Kevin Dempsey Sr, and the granddad, Old Man Dempsey -- are here together. The older man looks confused. He doesn't seem all there, if you know what I mean. When people pay their respects and ask him questions, he smiles but doesn't really say much.

The town supervisor, board members, attorney and town clerk arrange themselves on the dais.

The gavel goes down with a loud crack, and the Town Supervisor calls the meeting to order. He acknowledges that most are here for the hearing but that first there is some regular town business on the agenda, beginning with the Pledge of Allegiance.

All rise and place hands over hearts. We recite the pledge as if in a trance, chanting the words in monotone together.

Then we go on to sing the Star Spangled

Banner! One elderly man in the middle of the room wearing a Veterans of Foreign Wars cap starts the singing off loudly. "Oh say can you see," he sings with real feeling.

There is feeling in his voice, and I feel his allegiance strongly, to the point of tears.

After the pledge, there's a great shuffling and squeaking as people sit back down.

We move through the agenda. Motions are made. The motions are moved, seconded, and voted upon. Votes are recorded.

"With that, and before moving on to the bridge hearing, we'd like to ask Mr. And Mrs. Ford to please step to the front of the room," says the Town Supervisor.

A middle aged black couple standing at the back of the room walk to the front, where they're met at the foot of the dais by the entire town board. Dylan gets into position to get a photo of the group gathered.

"Mr. and Mrs. Ford," the Town Supervisor says, "As many of us know, you and your family recently received news that your son, Gerard Ford, made the ultimate sacrifice for our country. Today, the Town would like to extend our deepest condolences to you and your family for your loss and give you this Town Proclamation in his honor. In addition, a bronze plaque will be added in his name to our War Monument at

Veterans Park."

Dylan takes several pictures of the town board grouped with Mr. and Mrs. Ford.

"Would you like to say a few words, Mr. and Mrs. Ford?" the Supervisor asks.

Mr. Ford takes a step forward.

"Thank you. I'd like to thank the town for this kind recognition. It means the world to us and continues to sustain us. I know others in this town have children serving overseas now. This is news that none of us would ever want to receive, and it would be my prayer that no one else ever does. Gerald always put his heart and soul into anything he ever did, and we're sure he was a very fine soldier, someone that others could rely on. We're proud of him and appreciate this recognition and honor by the town. Thank you."

Mr. Ford takes a step back and stands next to his wife. He puts his arm around her shoulders as the audience gets on its feet to applaud them.

There is the great squeaking of seats. Without further ado, the Town Supervisor officially opens the bridge hearing. He turns the meeting over to a man in a suit standing at a flip chart.

I absolutely love the pointer, such a nice touch! Like a real live show.

Sitting behind the presenter up on the dais, the five elected officials read the room quietly with darting eyes and have side conversations among themselves.

The Supervisor directs those who wish to speak to form a line behind the podium.

Earl makes his way to the front of the line, saying loudly that he's got something to say, and unlike most assembled here today, he's an actual stakeholder with work to do. He can't be sitting at Town Hall all day like some of these people. People let him go ahead of them. He gets almost to the front, but Alexine refuses to budge.

Everyone knows Alexine's point of view, but standing there, she is filled with a new level of righteous energy. Up there, with her straight posture, she looks the very definition of propriety when she gives the opening speech.

Next comes Earl. Wow, he is worked up. Look at the big swagger as he steps up to the podium. He launches right in. He stands there, pointing fingers and practically spitting, promising to reassert what he sees as his natural born rights.

But first, he comments on the town honoring the fallen soldier. No one has given his brother any plaque. He uses a racial slur to describe the Fords and causes the Supervisor's gavel to come down with a loud crack. Throughout the room there is a low din and some chair squeaking. But Earl doesn't stop.

The gavel goes down again — crack! The Supervisor speaks slowly when he begs Earl to keep to the topic at hand, which is the highway extension and bridge. He asks that Earl's entire previous comment be struck from the record, and he reminds Earl that before he begins his statement for the record, he must state his full name and address like everyone else.

That slowed Earl's roll a little, temporarily.

It's key that he make a good case for the bridge.

Now, he lays into Alexine, on the record.

"I'd like to address the statement made by the first speaker, my old pal and neighbor," he says. "She's dead wrong about this thing, and in the good old days, we didn't have to listen to crazy old women like her yammer on about things and make a big fuss."

The gavel bangs.

"Alright, alright!" Earl continues. "God love her, she's a last surviving remnant of a certain breed. Alexine, bless your heart! But I've got news for ya, sooner or later this thing's gonna get built whether you like it or not. It just makes sense, which is something you women aren't naturally born with."

There goes the gavel again — crack!

"Mr. Butts," the Supervisor says. "Earl, please, please stick to the topic at hand and refrain from addressing anything or anyone in that tone, most especially our friends and neighbors. Would it help to collect your thoughts on the bridge plan and submit them in writing?"

"Most definitely not," Earl says. Earl continues, picking up where he left off, by asking by a show of hands how many assembled here today actually own any land along the proposed corridor. A few raise their hands. He asks how many have actually reviewed the plan, a copy of which he holds in his up-stretched hand. He bangs it back down on the podium and leans forward. "Has anyone read this thing cover to cover?"

There you go, Earl! He's really distinguishing himself now as someone who should have a say over this bridge. He says, "Isn't anyone else interested in a little thing called opportunity? Heck, I'm a big fat YES."

Bravo.

Oh wait, he's not done!

"Now I know a lot of you think farming is this wonderful thing. Let me tell you right now, if I could sell this land right now for enough to never have to farm again, I wouldn't think twice about it. I know what you all think of me. Something's not quite right," he says, pointing at his temple and looking around the room, his face contorted and red. "You think the draft board gave me a deferment for being not right up here. But look again. I'm the only able-bodied son in a farming family in a town that has lost its mind. It's a good thing I did stay behind to take care of my family's interests."

He looks around the room, daring a challenge. He continues, now pointing at himself with a thumb. "I'm the one who has to make these lazy farmhands work. I'm the one who has to collect rent from all the drifters and misfits along this godforsaken road you're all so worried about. But do you think anyone -- anyone! -- is worried about me and what I have to do? No, you all look down your noses at me. I mean, here you are, a big stuck up mob, headed up by her!" Earl looks straight at Alexine, who stares at him in horror.

The Supervisor cracks the gavel.

"Alright, alright. All I want to say is this: a lot of you here today don't want this highway and bridge deal, you dismiss it right out of hand. It's our only chance, our right, to a better life than scratching dirt year after year, and here you are handing out bronze plaques to..."

Then Earl looks straight at Mr. And Mrs. Ford.

The grieving parents of the fallen soldier are taken aback to say the least.

The gavel rings again in our ears.

That old veteran vocalist from the Star Spangled Banner gets up on his feet much faster than you'd think, his mouth hollering at Earl even before he can get his neck turned around to face him.

The Supervisor brings down the wooden gavel again and again as more people chime in and rise up in defense of the Fords. "Unfortunately, in the name of decorum, I'll have to ask that Mr. Butts be escorted from this hearing."

A group of full size men try to escort Earl out of the room. Earl's not budging, so they drag him out. It becomes a brawl.

Oh look, Dylan's getting photos of it all.

Wow. Just wow.

Earl is finally escorted out. People finally settle back down. It's over, really, in the sense that there remain only smaller stories to tell by much more timid folk who undoubtedly got roped into this thing by Alexine. They say what they came to say, but the real excitement -- we can feel their excitement -- is getting out of the room with their first person accounts of Earl being Earl.

The hearing goes on and on like this, and at one point we doze off, to be honest. When the Supervisor hits that gavel one last time to close the hearing, we jolt.

The chairs squeak, and folks file out. The town board and the planner pack up to leave as Dylan plies one or two of them with questions.

We go outside to get some fresh air. September is truly one of the most spectacular months of the year. The cool morning has turned into a warm summer day, and really, we'd rather be anywhere but Town Hall.

We catch a ride with Dylan on the way to the newspaper office building to see what he will write.

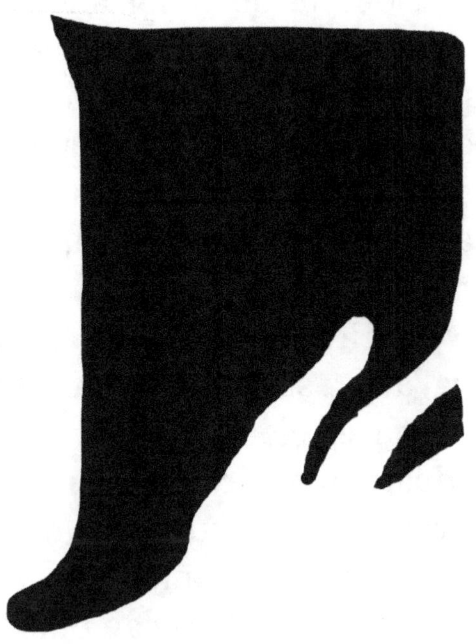

Chapter 30: Dylan Reports

We follow his car to the deli, then to the newspaper's office building. We follow him inside. In passing, a lady tells Dylan that his boss is out sick. Her voice trails off before she finishes speaking. Dylan drops off rolls of film to the art department, then sits at his desk.

Florescent bulbs flood the newsroom with artificial daylight. The buzzing light waves line our pockets with points.

Dylan gets out his notebook and opens his sandwich. It's a lovely sandwich with turkey and cheese, lettuce and tomato, mayo, salt and pepper on a fresh roll — and a pickle! Our mouths are watering as he takes a big bite and rolls a fresh sheet of blank paper into the typewriter.

Other typewriters in the room clack away, phones ring, and a second hand rotates around a large white-faced clock on the wall. There's a feverish industry in the room, and we can feel the pressure strongly as the countdown to the weekly deadline shortens by the minute.

Much depends on how Dylan puts the public hearing into words.

Dylan reads his notes as he eats his food.

Unfortunately, we can't read his handwriting. We must wait to see what he writes, and there's nothing we can do. He places his hands over the keys of the typewriter and glances at the clock. He stares at the paper in the typewriter and is about to strike the first letter of the first word when he abruptly stands up.

He crumples up the sandwich wrapping and throws it away. Then he goes to the bathroom. He sits back down and glances at his notes again. Nibbling on a fingernail, he stares at the paper in his typewriter again; the metal keys are arrayed in striking distance below the paper.

A good reporter's first words will convey
the essence of the entire story to such a degree
that even without reading the rest of the article,
readers will know what happened. By no means
is news writing easy. A newspaper article is not a
transcript. It's not an opinion column. But it is an
abridged version of what happened and requires
some editorializing as to what is important and
what is not in the grand scheme of things.

Dylan turns his gaze into the bright upper
space of the room as if to pluck words out of thin
air. When a phone rings, he's distracted. When
a colleague walks by, he's distracted. When
his teeth yank on a cuticle and it bleeds, he's
distracted.

Finally, he packs his notebook up and goes
home.

He finds Hannah hard at work in her
makeshift studio. He kisses her and goes up to
his quiet little room and shuts the door. We hear
precious little in the way of clacking and dinging.
He's still gathering his thoughts. So we look in at
what Hannah is painting, and really we're quite
impressed!

The abstraction, the colors, and the shapes
are much more sophisticated than we could have
imagined.

The next thing we know, the kids come home
from school, and they're restless and hungry,

rummaging through the kitchen cabinets and the refrigerator but finding nothing, at least nothing ready to eat.

Jack goes upstairs to his room and shuts the door. Lily interrupts her mother and comes away with nothing but the idea of going upstairs to ask her father what there is to eat. She knocks on his door. He gives her a hug and a kiss on the forehead, asks her how school was. She says it was good. She says she and Jack are starving and asks what's for dinner and if there's anything to eat. He gives her a kiss on her forehead and tells her to ask her mother, that he's working on a big story on a tight deadline and can't get involved in any of that today. She says she already did, and she said to ask him.

Dylan looks lovingly into the child's eyes and takes pity on her. He takes her downstairs to scrape something together to eat. It's a strange and inedible-looking concoction, but he adds ketchup and she eats it.

It's evening before we finally hear some clacking and dinging.

Oops, nope, there's the sound of paper getting yanked backward off the roller and crumpled up.

We settle into the empty bathtub for what promises to be a long night.

It's not comfortable, but we're so tired that we're soon drowsy.

I tell you, half in a dream state, that I know how this ends.

How does it end?

In tragedy.

Tragedy?

Yeah.

You sigh and dig out a small book from your satchel. You open it and read by moonlight.

I watch you for a minute, thinking about your nickname, the Ink Drinker. Big reader. I ask what you're looking for in books.

A good story, an escape, you say. It can give you a safe way to experience anything vicariously. Sometimes reading gives you a new way of seeing things or a solution. You love it when a writer puts into words an experience you've had, when you had no words for it. You're forever amazed at the deep connection that can be made with authors living and dead, from across time and space. You say it's the original multiverse of ideas.

Wow! That's really something. Well said.

You say that you've read many, many books, and you can tell me that a tragedy can easily be made into another kind of story by changing the course of the plot. Instead of a tragic ending, it could turn into something with a happy ending. Just steer the story a new way at key points. Writers can do anything.

That gives me something to think about. A new wave of gratitude washes over me for your help in navigating this mission together. It's with no small feeling of hope that I fall asleep to the tapping and dinging of Dylan's typewriter.

Chapter 31: Publication Day

It's a restless night filled until dawn with clacking and dinging, yanking and crumpling. By the time it goes quiet and the lights go out in the Bogle house, it's nearly dawn.

I think I can speak for us both when I say how crickety my whole body feels from sleeping in the tub.

"Hey kids!" Dylan shouts upstairs as he's getting ready to take his work to the office. He's tired and grouchy. "Kids! Let's go! You're gonna miss the bus! Aw, damn it all, there it goes! Kids! Aw, damn it, not today!"

The bus leaves without Jack and Lily.

"Alright," he hollers. "I'll drive you but we have to leave, like, now!"

Hannah comes to the bedroom door, tying her robe and pushing back her hair. "Will you stop shouting?"

Jack and Lily are like zombies the entire way to school. School starts very early, and they've had no breakfast. They have no lunch with them, either. Dylan is very focused on getting to work and delivering his stories.

He drops them off.

The boss is still out sick, the secretary tells Dylan in passing. "Do your best," she says.

The building is sheer pandemonium. We can feel it.

Dylan drops off his stories directly to the art department, checks on his photos, and spends the rest of the day working on editing and layout.

Now we wait to read in print his treatment of the public hearing. What did he write and how will it affect the bridge?

A draft lands on his desk.

I nearly have a heart attack when I see the cover. It's a big, ugly picture of Earl Butts mid-swing and the headline "Highway Hearing Comes to Blows."

Oh dear Lord.

Good grief.

Then there's a Page 2 feature story about
the couple who lost their son in the war with
photos of the young hero and his family, and the
beginning of another story about controversy
at the local draft board. Apparently the board
is accused of sending minorities to war and
excusing others based on things like bone spurs.

Across the spread, on Page 3, the cover story
about the bridge hearing continues, including a
second photo of Earl speaking at the podium and
pointing at the Fords with a vicious look in his
eye.

Turning the page to the next spread are two
full pages about the man behind the push for
the bridge, who we recognize as One. There he is
in all his glory! In the biggest photo, he wears a
silly hat at his own parade on his estate. His face
shows that he is both drunk and out of his mind.

Dylan's byline is on all of these top stories,
pages 1 through 5. His and only his byline is all
over them.

The papers hit newstands and mailboxes
throughout the region. Gears turn, wheels spin,
and phones ring. I can feel it strongly, but I
cannot see it, touch it, smell it, or hear it. I know
that a verdict is coming. My breathing is shallow.

My heart races. I feel sick. I may pass out.

You tell me to take deep breaths. Ready? In. Hold. Exhale. Slowly, slowly. Again. That's right. Good. Now try this: name one thing I see?

A desk.

One thing I hear?

A humming sound.

One thing I smell?

Newsprint.

Good.

We sit with Dylan at his desk for a while as he reads his articles through. He brings his notes back to the art department and returns with a cup of coffee to read the national and regional newspapers on his desk. Local news happens in the context of a much larger news universe.

The local, national and international news are part of the same big wave hitting around the globe. Watergate is in full swing. Reporters are battling for basic facts in the face of threats and denials. Every small victory adds a piece to the puzzle. It's a strong calling, and Dylan feels he belongs in this group. We can feel it strongly.

When the boss returns the day after publication, still under the weather, we get the first real indication of how the articles are hitting.

Chapter 32: Dylan Pays the Piper

"Well when you give someone enough rope, they will hang themselves," says the Editor to Dylan the minute they encounter each other in the building. "My office!"

The Editor, a pale man with red blotchy skin and a big stomach, waves a hand at the seat in front of his desk. He wipes his nose with a hankie from his pocket. "Your stories are making quite a ruckus."

"Really? Which one?" Dylan asks.

"All of 'em." The Editor looks at Dylan over his bifocals. He isn't smiling. "I'm out sick — sick mind you! — and the Publisher, along with the lawyer for the Butts family, along with the head of the draft board, along with half this town, are calling me up on my home phone and stopping me on the street."

"That's strange. I haven't heard anything," Dylan says.

"It would be nice if I could take a couple of days off without the shit hitting the fan. This photo of one of our region's most elite and esteemed members, with his hat on crooked and a turkey leg in his mouth, seated among a clownish brigade of buffoons in full dress, that shouldn't have gone in the paper, let alone the whole article. Who told you to do an expose on him?"

"But he's been the one pushing for this bridge! I've been trying for a long time to interview him, and I finally managed to get through the gate with his big event over there. I finally got his spokesman, a guy named Steve, to speak with me..."

"Not very becoming, though, is it? You picked a fight with a person with unlimited resources who enjoys crushing people under foot. We're under a lot of pressure as it is, we don't need this!

What the hell were you thinking? Were you even thinking at all about anyone but your own career and your slavish dedication to the so-called truth? I don't know how many times I've gone over this kind of thing with you. I've really tried to help you understand this business. You should know better by now than to be so reckless."

Dylan is dumbfounded.

The Editor looks at Dylan pitifully. "Look, what's this really all about? You're a talented guy, but we have to go back and forth quite a bit. I don't know how many times I've had to save your butt and everyone else's by not letting something get printed. You don't see that though. I'm out sick and you take your chance to get some things past me?"

"No, I'm just trying to give readers a flavor for what's happening, give them the whole story, not some watered down version..." Dylan says, but the Editor puts his hand up to silence him.

"I liked your writing clips. But you should know better, you really should. We're not in the business of raising hell in news coverage. That's for me and our Editorial Board to do based on our long experience here in this community. This is a business!"

"I wasn't trying, I mean, I thought I wrote a straightforward, I mean, that's exactly what happened..."

"Yes, well, there's what happened, and then there's what happens."

Dylan looks confused.

"The Chamber of Commerce President called me," the Editor continues, "and said that his statement at the hearing could have been read another way. It left some wiggle room both ways. You took the story the way you wanted it to go, and you didn't listen for anything else."

Dylan thinks about that.

The Editor continues. "And printing Earl Butts's racist remarks word-for-word, what the hell was that? And again, very unbecoming photographs!"

"That's what Earl said. That's what he did," Dylan says.

"Well, we don't have to pile on by printing every burp and fart that people make. What did Earl ever do to you? Isn't he your landlord for Christ's sake? Is there a problem I should've known about?"

Dylan looks dumbfounded. "Not at all. I only reported what he said, without fear or favor."

"Your questioning of members of the draft board about who gets deferments and who doesn't was not well received. These are esteemed members of the community, that's why they're picked for this thankless job. And you want to go write an expose?"

"Earl Butts and the Fords mentioned the draft in my interviews with them. I simply did some research and found out there's a story there," Dylan says.

"Well I would say that you've managed to paint a very unflattering and controversial portrait of our town, and a lot of important people don't like it, to say the least. And I'm the one who has to hear about it when I get back to the office after being out sick. Just between you and me, I've had some very nasty anonymous calls about your profile of the Ford family," the Editor says, looking more sympathetic but now defeated. "The bottom line is, you've stirred up a heap of trouble. It's going to take the newspaper a while to get back on an even keel with this community. I'm sorry, but I have to let you go," the Editor says.

"But I was only doing my job," Dylan says.

"If you thought your job was to turn this town inside out, then you did. But it isn't. And I'm sorry I wasn't here to stop it, but you put yourself and this paper way out on a limb. Firing you would signal a correction, and we'll still have to smooth things over for a while."

They sit in silence for a few moments.

"Okay," Dylan says and stands up. "I actually thought you'd like my articles, you talk a lot about publishing the truth. That was the truth as best I could tell it."

"The truth? The truth is I've lost my patience for this type of rookie crap," says the Editor. "Talk to Rita in Accounting, then go on home."

At home, Dylan finds Hannah sitting in the kitchen with a cup of coffee and a cigarette. He tells her what happened. She listens, holding her stomach and groaning.

When the kids get home from school, Dylan tells them he lost his job.

The kids are dumbfounded and quiet.

Dylan answers their questions, but as concerns the future, there are no answers yet. Lily comforts Dylan, Hannah takes to her bed, and Jack leaves the house, letting the screen door bang closed behind him.

I tell you there is a feeling, I can feel it very strongly.

What kind of feeling.

Bad. A bad one. Very bad.

I open my satchel and a dispatch titled "TRUTH?" is right there on top. I place it in Dylan's pocket next to his final check from the newspaper.

Hannah stays in bed, in the fetal position. Dylan goes out of his skull, just going over it all in his head, pulling his hair out, biting his nails to the quick. Lily goes to bed early but can't sleep. Jack stays out all night.

We spend another uncomfortable night in the
tub. You open your book and make the best of it.
I open a notebook and jot down some notes for
the report and ponder how this all plays out. The
window is open, and cold night air seeps in.

In desperation, I send a message to HQ
asking for someone to come get us out of here.
Eventually, I fall asleep.

In the early morning, there's a very loud bang.

Chapter 33: The Accident

Lily's the first one to the front window. She bolts out the door. She runs right back in, "Dad, come quick!"

Dylan comes out from the bedroom.

"Dad! It's a potato truck! It crashed! Look! There's potatoes everywhere!" Lily runs right back out again.

Hannah and Dylan both go out the front door and make their way down the driveway toward the accident. The truck lays on its side. Dylan walks to the front to look through the windshield. A man in a plaid shirt starts to move inside the cab.

"Kevin? Is that you?" Dylan asks. "Jesus! Are you alright?" Dylan climbs to the driver side and opens the door like a hatch.

The entire region's emergency services come. They check Kevin Dempsey Jr out for injuries. He says he lost control when he thought he saw a ghost in a bride's veil out in front of Alexine's.

The truck is extracted from the scene.

Potatoes are indeed everywhere — in the road, in the ditch, and in the Bogles's yard. Lily gathers them up and puts them into brown paper bags from the grocery store. The bags grow and multiply! She makes a sign to sell the bags for a quarter apiece.

Word gets out, and soon ladies pull up and leave with lots of potatoes and gossip to share around town.

Potato dishes dance in my head. Mashed potatoes, scalloped potatoes, potatoes au gratin, potato perogies, meat and potatoes, hash brown potatoes, French fries, home fries, and other earthly delights. I'm comforted by the idea of these potato dishes in spite of the tragedy unfolding before us.

Who should show up at the Bogles but Alexine

herself. "That's no bride he saw, it was me!" She explains that she was standing in front of her farmstand still wearing her bee bonnet. He was going too fast, and he barrelled right toward her. When she'd raised her arms in alarm, he lost control completely. She gets right up close to Kevin with that keen nose of hers and asks him if he's been drinking.

He doesn't say anything. He just hangs his head.

She tells him he'd better straighten up, he's got a baby on the way. There's big important stuff going on in the world, and he's going to need all of his faculties. She picks out two bags of Lily's potatoes and holds out a dollar.

Lily says, "Oh no, that's okay. No charge."

"Well thank you very much, young lady." Alexine gets in her truck and drives away.

Jack returns home and wants to know what the heck is happening. Lily relays the whole incident in detail.

After all the emergency services are gone, and after giving Kevin some coffee, the entire Bogle family walks Kevin home. We follow.

Chapter 34: Francesca Leaves

We arrive at the Dempsey home later morning. The Bogles head back home. Kevin walks in and takes off his shoes. He finds Francesca laying on her side across the couch watching television. There is laughing and clapping on the show she's watching, but she stares vacantly at the blue light.

He walks silently across the room to the stairs. After shaving and changing, Kevin comes back down and sits near Francesca.

Francesca gets up off the couch, goes upstairs, and comes back down carrying a suitcase. She walks past Dylan. She takes her pocketbook and car keys off the kitchen counter and goes to the door. Kevin catches her arm.

"Take your hands off of me," she says. "Word travels real fast around here, and I heard all about what happened."

He frees her, and she opens the back door. It only partially opens. Kevin's socked foot is in the way, and his hand is on the door above.

"You're not gonna stop me this time, Kevin."

"What are you gonna do, just leave? Frannie, come on. Where you gonna go? What about the baby?"

"I don't know. All I know is I can't take another minute of this. Earl was right, I am going to waste around here."

"Another minute of what? Is this because of the accident? And I can't believe you're bringing up what Earl Butts says!"

"I'm not going to fight with you anymore, Kevin. You know damned well what this is all about. Move out of my way."

"Baby, please. What did I do?"

"Don't. I'm not arguing with you."

Kevin steps aside.

Francesca walks to her car, starts it, puts it in

drive, and steps on the gas. A cloud of dust rises into the air and trails her car all the way to the end of the driveway.

Francesca comes to where Kevin drove the potato truck into the ditch, right outside the Bogles' place. Lily sits at her makeshift potato stand. Francesca pulls over and stops the car.

Francesca looks around, her hands on the wheel. Lily comes up to her passenger window.

"Hi Lily."

"Hi Mrs. Dempsey. How's Mr. Dempsey?"

"Him? He's fine."

"Lucky he didn't get killed!"

"Yeah."

"Mom's here, you wanna come in?"

"Is she?" Francesca leans and peers up the driveway in time to see Hannah walking toward them. "I guess just for a minute."

Francesca takes her purse and gets out.

Lily goes back to her potato stand by the side of the road. Francesca and Hannah greet each other and head into the house.

In the kitchen, Francesca settles at the kitchen table while Hannah spoons instant coffee from a jar into two cups.

The women sit across from each other, and their eyes meet. The kettle whistles, Hannah pours, and they mix in milk and sugar.

Hannah says, "You must be very upset."

"I guess you could say that," Francesca says. "You don't even know the whole story."

"What happened?"

"We had a big fight last night. He came home from the bar late and he stank."

"Stank?"

"Literally stank, like sweat and booze were oozing out of his pores between farming and drinking. He thought he was just going to come in, kick off his shoes and get into bed with me, and I lost it."

"Oh dear."

"I don't know if it's the pregnancy hormones or what, but I really lost it." Francesca says, her eyes welling with tears. Shakily, she moves her cup to her lips and takes a small sip of hot coffee. It soothes her instantly, and she takes another bigger sip. Then she puts her cup down. "Kevin drove that truck off the road and lost all those potatoes and almost got killed. If he wasn't still a little drunk or hungover, it never would've happened. It makes me so mad! I'm just sick and tired of the whole thing."

"I'm sure you are...."

"We were already fighting about money without him being a complete jackass and crashing the truck!" Francesca says. "He goes where he wants, does whatever he wants, and I'm there at the house, day and night, never going anywhere. I'm going crazy."

Hannah tisks and sighs.

Francesca continues, "And life with Kevin is nothing like I thought it would be. We used to be so in love! He was my Prince Charming, taking me away from my crazy family to be with him and create an enchanted life together. I honestly don't know what happened. But I do know that ever since I got pregnant, he's been different."

"Oh come on, honey, that's probably just the hormones talking again."

"Maybe, but I really have gotten positively fat! He doesn't want me anymore." Francesca looks past her friend out the kitchen window above the sink.

The room is still. It's that empty stillness when enchantment ends but nothing yet takes its place. It's possible to get lost in that space forever.

"Well if that's how you feel, then that's how you feel. What are you gonna do?"

"I'm gonna get back in my car and drive. I'll be able to think better driving, if I can get away from here."

Hannah sighs, "Do you need anything? Do you have money?"

"Not much, just what I had in my purse. Like I said, I can't think. I've been so stupid."

"OK, you just sit here and catch your breath, let me see what I can rummage up for you. Be right back, okay?

"OK."

When Hannah returns, she puts a zipped pouch into Francesca's hand. "Now here, you take this. It's enough for you to drive, sleep and eat for a few days. You come back when you're good and ready."

"I can't take this from you, Dylan just got fired, and..."

"Yes you can, I insist. We'll manage. Right now I'm more worried about you," says Hannah.

Francesca sobs. "You're so good to me. You're one of the few people I've ever known who's been really good to me."

"And here," says Hannah, flourishing some clothes on hangers, "Would you like to take a few pretty things with you to wear?"

"Really? These are so pretty!" Francesca gets up and touches the sleeve of a blue and white floral blouse. She holds a pretty red polka dotted blouse up against her chest for size.

"Go ahead into my room, try things on, take what you like, freshen up for your trip, take your time."

When Francesca comes back, she's much cheered. Hannah grabs a straw hat off of a hook on the wall by the front door. "Here, take this too, you'll look gorgeous in it, and it'll bring you good luck. Plus it'll keep the sun out of your eyes."

"Thanks," says Francesca as she puts it on and the two go out the door and down the driveway together.

They say their goodbyes, and Francesca gets in her car, closes the door, and starts her engine.

I must say there's a sense of sisterhood between the two women.

Francesca's red tail lights come on against the lengthening shadows of the day, and we feel compelled to stay with her awhile.

Some way down the road, Francesca's hands shake so badly she has to pull over to the side of the road. She puts the car in park, leans on the wheel, and sobs. She cries out and hits the steering wheel with the palm of her hand. She reaches into her bag for a tissue and dries her tears.

You pull a dispatch out of your satchel with a map of the island and lay it across her dashboard.

She turns on the radio and adjusts the dial to a local station. She pulls back onto the road, then onto the highway, where her vehicle joins a river of lights.

The radio reception gets spotty as she goes further and further from home. The signage is confusing, but she keeps driving, into the falling night.

Later, hers in the only vehicle on the road and a late night radio DJ asks how she's doing. She glances at her gas gauge, which is nearly empty. There's a road sign advertising food and lodging. She takes the exit.

Francesca gets settled into this rather incredible motel with neon lights, blinking bulbs, and televisions. There's an all-night diner attached! Our pockets are buzzing with points.

At dawn, you and I hitch a ride with three different drivers back to Sumditch Avenue, a trip that takes much longer getting back than than it took getting there.

Chapter 35: Francesca Hangs Up

In Francesca's kitchen, the whole family is there, except of course for Francesca.

Kevin Jr looks haggard, but he's cleaned up and sober. Kevin Sr is there with him. And so are his grandparents, Old Man Dempsey and Grandma Rose.

Grandma Rose serves the men coffee while they wait for breakfast at the table. "While you boys are out, I'll man the phone in case Francesca calls. And I'll get some lunch and dinner going for later."

I tell you, quietly, I'd like to comment on Francesca's kitchen if I may.

Go ahead, you say.

Nothing makes sense. Utensils, plates, cups, glasses — nothing is where it would be most handy. Drawers and cabinets are all a'jumble. And not to be rude, but the floors, counters and stove top could use a real scrubbing.

When the cast iron pan is hot, Grandma Rose sprinkles it with water from her fingertips to make sure it's hot enough. The water droplets sizzle on impact. She adds oil to the pan, dips a piece of bread in egg batter, and lays it in the pan. She repeats this many times until each man has a big stack of French toast, plus a small stack for herself.

The men finish and walk out to the barn.

Old Man Dempsey mounts a loaded potato truck. Kevin Sr tries to talk him out of driving it while Kevin Jr looks down and jams his fists into his jeans pocket.

The old man waves off his son, and that's the end of that discussion. He puts it in gear and takes off.

The old man is positively determined. I feel it strongly that today there would be no stopping him. Positively heroic. Thinking of Alexine and

Old Man Dempsey, I have to say, that is one durable generation.

The farm view is sensational, with big billowing clouds parading right overhead.

Kevin Sr waves at his dad and pats his son on the shoulder. Then they get to work on harvesting because when it's time, there's no waiting. Even if your life is falling apart.

Wow, what a team. Truly, it's a marvel to behold. Such strength, such competence, such love. Here is a family pulling together.

Brinnnngggg! The phone actually rings.

Our pockets fill with points! What a fantastically loud ring that is, that bell is glorious. It's cheerful yet alarming at the same time. It rings and rings while Grandma Rose wipes her hands and gets to it.

She picks up the receiver and says, "Hello!" She repeats, "Hello?..." She looks out the kitchen window and listens hard. "Hello, honey is that you?"

We get up close to listen, too. We hear nothing at all, then a click.

Grandma Rose hangs up and takes a few things from the refrigerator and cabinets, shaking her head.

Here comes Earl, speeding along Sumditch Avenue. It's hard to miss! He turns into the Bogles' driveway across the way.

We go see what fresh hell Earl is dishing out today.

Chapter 36: Earl Visits the Bogles

Earl arrives outside the Bogle's home in his usual plume of dust. He gets out of his truck, slams its door, and goes right up to the front door. "Hello?" he says toward an open window.

Earl knocks, then opens the door part way. "Hello?" He puts one foot in. "Hello?"

Hannah comes into the living room from her bedroom. She is disheveled to say the least, pulling a large cardigan across her chest. She startles to find the hulking figure of Earl standing there in her small living room — in dirty clunky work boots no less!

"Morning, Mam, is your husband home?"

"No he's not," she says.

"Well will you give him a message for me?"

"Alright, but let's step outside," Hannah says, looking at his shoes.

Earl lumbers out the front door and steps onto the ground just beyond the porch. He turns back to Hannah and puts one boot back up on the porch. He says, "I've heard that your, uh, family circumstances have changed, and I'm hereby giving you notice that any failure to pay your rent right on time will result in a speedy eviction."

Lily comes outside, followed by Jack.

Jack stands next to Hannah, arms at his side, and says, "Mom? What's going on?"

"Mr. Butts is just delivering a message for your dad." Hannah crosses her arms. She, Jack, and Lily all stand there, staring at Earl.

"Ok then, I can cross that off my list," Earl says and turns to go. But he's not done. "Ya know," he says. "You people, the next place you get to, might want to think about minding your own business a little more than you do. Every last one of you's been a thorn in my side since you got here, starting with your husband butting his nose into this bridge deal and writing all that nasty stuff about me and taking those nasty pictures and putting them in the paper like that."

"That's his job," Hannah says.

"Well, not any more I guess. And you there, boy, don't you have nothing better to do than always lurking around down at your girlfriend's like you live there?"

"Keep my son out of this," says Hannah. Earl is about to continue but she talks over him. "Don't you talk to my son like that."

"What I do or what Veronica does is none of your business," Jack says.

Hannah jumps right in, saying, "That's enough. Mr. Butts your message is received and you should leave now."

Earl turns his attention to her again. "What is it with the women on this road lately? If I didn't know better, I'd think there's some kind of witch thing going on around here. I see you and your new best friend Francesca Dempsey over there chattering and laughing away all the damn time. Look how that's turning out, her pregnant and all, leaving Kevin like that. I bet you had something to do with that."

Hannah says, "Do not speak to me like that."

"Well, I hope you're happy," he says. Turning back to Jack, he says, "And as a matter of fact, young man, it is my concern. I'm the man of the house down there, and I do have some concerns.

Know what I mean?"

"No, I don't know what you mean," Jack says.

"Lady, you do know that your kids practically live at that old witch's, right? Don't you worry that Alexine's gonna cook 'em for dinner some night when the cupboards are empty?"

"That's enough!" Hannah says. "We're not going to stand here, especially with the children, listening to your nasty, vile diatribe." She turns to go in the house.

"Well, lady, you've got quite a loud mouth, haven't you? What are you, Mam?" Earl looks Hannah up and down. He turns up his nose. "I mean, where are your people from? I heard you're a Jewesssss? You've got that skin tone."

Jack steps forward. Hannah pulls him back.

"Watch yourself, city boy," says Earl. "Things are done a little differently out here in the country. You'll see."

In a low, calm voice, Hannah says, "I have never in all my life met a ruder, stupider man than you, and I've met a lot of people. All kinds of people from all kinds of places. You are by far the worst. Coming here with your big dumb message at a time when our family's in serious trouble."

"Well now, you all did that to yourselves. I have to do what I have to do with respect to collecting rent that is due on time. Your husband comes to town and sticks his nose everywhere

it don't belong. He writes all that bad stuff
about a person from this town right in our own
newspaper, tries to bury that bridge deal along
the way. Why?"

"Well you did that to yourself, Mr. Butts, with
your own outrageous behavior at the hearing,"
Hannah says.

"Ha! Ya know, I asked myself, 'What'd I
ever do to your husband?' All I did was very
kindly rent him and his little family a place to
live. Well now I've got some news for you folks.
Everyone in this town is more behind me now
than ever thanks to the way your husband treated
me. I should thank him. I mean, he really put
himself out there. But if you don't believe me
you can read all about it in the newly improved
newspaper now featuring better reporters."

Hannah says, "I wonder if you'd talk like this
if my husband were here, or are you just a big
coward picking on women and children."

"Well I'd be all too glad to speak to your
husband. Where is he exactly? I'll go find him."

"He's not here," says Lily, stepping forward.
"He's out looking for a new job. Mr. Butts, what if
I walk you to your truck. Would that be okay?"

Hannah and Jack reach for her and pull her
toward them.

"Mr. Butts, go back to your truck, get in, and
get out of here before I call the police."

Earl regards Lily, momentarily disarmed.

"Well young lady, you're about the only one with any manners in this family," Earl says and walks to his truck by himself, gets in, and pulls out in a plume of dust.

Later, Dylan comes home. He goes into the bedroom with Hannah and shuts the door. It's one of those conversations probably. We hear him talk, but the sound is muffled. I put my ear up to the door, and I can sort of hear him say something about getting blacklisted from here to someplace called Kalamazoo. "No one will hire me," he says.

In a while, Dylan opens the door. He goes in the kitchen to start one of his famous concoctions.

Lured by the smell of something cooking, Jack and Lily come downstairs.

Dylan announces that the family may be moving back into the city. He's going to try to find work there, and when he does, he'll come back for them. He asks if there's anything he can bring back.

Hannah asks if he'd take slides of her new paintings to galleries. Jack wants magazines and records. Lily offers Dylan her potato money.

"Thanks kiddo, but you hold onto it," he says. "Help Mom out. Jack, you too."

After the meal, he packs a bag and leaves.

Chapter 37: Birds Eye View

It's hard to pinpoint when this wave of calamity crested and began its relentless cascade. Was it the bridge hearing? Was it the late summer storm at Alexine's when her hair seemed to be alight? Was it the moment Alexine snapped at Veronica and Darla, causing the kids to pull away from her and her world.

You and I decide that tonight, we'll camp out on Alexine's beach cliff with the glorious views.

There, we'll be able to stretch our limbs and watch the sun set and rise. The pace has picked up, and we need the clarity that only a good night's sleep can bestow.

To get to the cliff, we go through the wooded path to Alexine's, pass by her driveway, and go on up the dirt road. In passing, I assess that Alexine's harvest is in full swing. Migrant workers in straw hats crouch in her fields and climb her trees, bringing in baskets of produce.

The old woman herself tends to the beeswax, honey, floral bouquets, soaps, sachets, and candles that hold the most magic. Duke and Greta are well.

The dirt road is lined with sweet wildflowers and pepper and mustard scented weeds. We spot small slivers of the deep blue sea beyond the cliff.

We hurry to catch what will surely be a spectacular sunset. The sky is orange to the west.

The roar of the sea grows louder the closer we get. The sea is kicking up. Winds gust across the surface in bursts, and we track their movement.

We cross the grassy knoll where we had that wonderful picnic and step up to a clear view of the sea from up high. Near the edge, the height makes us both dizzy. I look down in time to notice that the cliffs have eroded! One more step and we might have fallen down the steep ravine and cracked our skulls on the boulders below. I pull you back in the nick of time.

Wow, this truly is the best sunset I've ever seen. What a majestic display! Its mirror image shines on the surface of the water, more than doubling the effect.

You agree, it's spectacular.

Gradually, the great orange orb sinks into the sea, and the world drains of color. The horizon line is backlit in yellow neon for a few moments. Then it's gone. Gradually, darkness sets in.

Now we can't see the water at all, we can only hear it. An autumn chill sets in.

We craft a temporary campsite for the night and insulate our clothes with fallen leaves. A new moon soon rises, and we lay down under a dome of familiar constellations. I think about the Org and wonder what is happening back on the mainland, back in so-called civilization. I wonder why they haven't been able to extract us from this terrible situation.

Of course, as you rightly point out, the night sky is not actually a dome. On this dark clear night, we're looking out at infinite dark space itself speckled with stars. We may be creatures of daylight, but at night we can see the truth.

In the Outer Lands Archipelago, nights are darker and the skies clearer. I feel very strongly, I can feel it, intoxicated and paralyzed by its terrible beauty and awesome scale. Lying down on Earth itself, I'm not feeling grounded now. Everything is in motion. If I can't stop thinking about it, I'll probably panic. I think to myself that the truth is that we might be stuck here on this island forever because I don't know if I can complete this mission.

You snore, and it comforts me. I snap right out of the thought pattern. I close my eyes, take deep breaths and imagine the cliff holding me. Eventually I fall asleep.

In the morning, my doubts from the night fade as the sun comes up. Now it's a question of what to do next.

The first thing we do is we go downtown in order to kill two birds with one stone. The idea is to shake off whatever this doubt is I'm harboring while at the same time find out what's really happening around town since the bridge hearing.

Chapter 38: The News

We post ourselves right inside the deli on Main Street. We drool over egg, bacon and cheese sandwiches on rolls, fresh pastries, and hot coffee. Stacks of newspapers and magazines on a display rack reflect the platinum autumn light.

Everyone who walks in grabs a copy of the local newspaper. All around us, people are talking about the bridge controversy.

Our own reading of the local paper tells

us a lot. There's a new reporter. People have already forgotten about Dylan Bogle. The bridge controversy has taken a turn. The merits of the project have gained traction. Earl has gone from being reviled to revered as a native son who speaks for the locals, albeit not always eloquently, for which he is forgiven. Forgiveness is as much a joy to give as it is to receive, for it lets us all be perfectly imperfect.

There's a photo of him with the gang at the club, posing together for a charity event. Well if that isn't a ringing endorsement for Earl I don't know what is.

There's an editorial throwing Dylan Bogle under the bus without mentioning names or specifics. It's artfully done.

There's a letter to the editor from Earl himself (no doubt with a little help) objecting to ill treatment and demanding respect and restitution for himself and his family. He reminds everyone that on top of everything else, his brother is a wounded war veteran, and his family is undergoing unimaginable hardship right now. Still, he will continue to fight for what's right.

Earl goes on to say the highway extension and bridge aren't the end of the world that the "chicken little" naysayers claim; it could be a new beginning. Old Puritans are being too dramatic. Heritage and way of life? Not nearly as precious as some pretend they are, and the need for better sources of income than farming is real. Earl says he's doing exactly what people expected he would: selling his family's properties to make way for the proposed highway.

And there are more letters to the editor in favor of the bridge proposal than against. People are defending property rights and the Butts family's reputation. There's local unity against "outsiders."

In other words, blowback from Dylan's heroics amounts to a big win for Earl.

Even Alexine has one or two corrections to make in Dylan's reporting. She writes that although she resents the bad language, rude behavior, and mean nicknames used at the public hearing, she deeply regrets the newspaper's decision to repeat it all verbatim. She reiterates that if a bridge is coming, it'll be over her dead body. She is taking measures to preserve her farm for posterity. Hers is really the only real bridge opposition in this week's edition.

Chapter 39: Kevin Goes To Francesca

With the tide turning in favor of the bridge project, with Earl taking steps to sell, and Alexine taking steps to preserve her farm forever, we wonder what the Dempseys will do. We go next to their farm to see which way they're leaning.

We get there as Kevin Jr steps through his kitchen door on a lunch break. Grandma Rose has left him a short note and a casserole on the counter. He digs in with the serving spoon without so much as a plate. He plows through fully two-thirds of the baking dish before putting the spoon down. He gulps down two large glasses of iced tea. He's about to go back out when the phone rings.

Bringgg! Bringgg!

Uh, what a wonderful sound.

He picks up.

"Hello?"

"Frannie? Oh my God, Frannie... Baby, are you okay?..."

"But I do...I do understand."

"This farm won't bury our love alive... I won't let that happen."

"Farmer's wife? How can you take that out on me though? You knew what I was..."

"I'd never let you disappear."

"I need you so much..."

"I'm sorry, I... (sobbing)"

"I know we can figure it all out."

"I promise you..."

"I've been thinking about it, talking it over with Dad and my grandparents. I want to talk it over with you, see what you think."

"Where are you?...Where?... No kidding, all the way up there?"

"Please, please, please. Let me come get you."

"Babe, how could you leave me like that?... I keep asking myself where things went wrong for us. But it doesn't matter. Nothing matters but being together."

"You're not gonna be lonely. Never again. No."

"No more going through the motions of what's expected."

"Frannie, I love you. We love each other, right? I'm never gonna take my eyes off of you. Please, let me come get you and bring you home..."

"Okay... okay babe... I'll... I'll be there as soon as I can."

We go with him. By evening, we get to that same gloriously lit up motel where we'd last seen her. He pulls up in front of Francesca's room, gets out of the truck, and knocks quietly on her door. He opens the door, walks in, and closes it softly behind him.

We spend the night riding the motel's arches of lights, filling our pockets with points and shouting from the rooftops at this one piece of good news in this avalanche of catastrophe.

In the morning, the couple enjoys big hardy breakfast platters at the adjoining diner. They're like newlyweds again. Kevin fills their gas tanks at the gas station, and we begin the long ride back to Sumditch Avenue.

On the last stretch home to the Dempsey farm, I notice the Bogle's house and how it gives me an empty feeling. Yes, I'm troubled to see it.

Chapter 40: Lean Times

You have to agree there's something about the Bogle's brown clapboard house that's gone dull and gray. You've passed as many houses as I have, and we can tell a lot just by looking. It looks like no one's home. The yard is unkempt.

We come up to a stopped school bus with its lights blinking, and we wait as Jack and Lily get off the bus. They walk up their driveway and into a dark, quiet house. We find Hannah in bed under the blankets in the fetal position. An autumn chill is in the air.

Jack turns on the lights in the kitchen. He opens and closes the kitchen cabinets and fridge. "Mom, there's nothing to eat! We're starving!"

Hannah doesn't answer.

It's cereal and milk apparently. Jack slams everything onto the table and sits down to eat a heaping bowl. Lily sits timidly across from him, cowered by his hungry temper, and pours herself what's left of the cereal and milk.

When they're done, they're still hungry.

"Let's go get something else to eat," Lily says.

"With what money?" Jack wants to know.

"My potato money."

"And how are we supposed to get there exactly?"

"Bikes?" Lily says.

"Okay, come on. Get your potato money and let's go."

On the way, they stop at Florence's. Veronica and Darla are home, and they're hungry, too. They scrape together a little bit of money, and they go along with the Bogles.

The four of them bike all the way to the grocery store and back, arriving back to the Bogles at dark. They've spent all of the money.

With just a can opener and a pan, they're all able to feast on ravioli till they can't take another bite, soon followed by chocolate bars, cookies, and soda. They leave the pot and all of their dishes in the sink.

Jack goes to take Veronica and Darla home, and Lily wants to go, too. He says no and leaves without her. Hannah's room is dark, so Lily goes up to her own room. She falls asleep doing her homework in bed.

We bunk in Jack's room. He doesn't come home all night.

Lily oversleeps and misses the school bus. Jack rolls in mid-morning and goes straight to bed.

At midday, Lily wanders out of the house, through the woods, and over to Alexine's. Duke and Greta are happy to see her, but Alexine doesn't seem to be. She doesn't even stop working to talk to Lily. Without her colorful sun hat, the old woman's wrinkled flesh and wild gray hair age her many years since the last time Lily saw her.

"Well, look who it is," Alexine says. "What brings you around?"

"Oh, I was just out walking and thought I'd stop over," Lily says.

"Really?" Alexine says, doubtfully. "And shouldn't you be in school?"

"I missed the bus," Lily says.

"You missed the bus? So you're just not going

to school then? I don't allow truants here."

"I'm sorry, I didn't know what to do, and Jack wasn't home, and Mom's…"

"What do you mean, 'Jack wasn't home'? Where was he? Did he miss the bus, too?"

"I don't know where he went, but he missed the bus, too."

"Ah, well, I can see we've arrived at the place where I knew we'd be when I made the mistake of introducing you to those girls. If you're not careful, things could get much, much worse than they already are!"

"Well, Dad got fired from his job and he went into the city to find work, and…"

"Into the city? Good heavens! And where's your mother?"

"She's not feeling well. She's been in bed a lot."

"Good heavens."

"Actually, I was wondering…"

"Well, if you and your brother are looking for work now, you made it clear that you weren't interested, and I hired some hands for the season."

"Okay," Lily says.

"You go on home now," Alexine says. "You can check back with me again after you and your brother have gotten yourselves back to school. That's number one."

"Okay," Lily says. She turns around and starts back home the way she came.

"And don't come back wearing that kind of get-up you have on. It might be what today's youth are wearing but it's not the right attire for working on a farm!" Alexine calls after her.

Lily glances back and hurries away.

Duke stands between Alexine and the retreating girl, wagging his tail for her to come back.

The next day after school, Lily changes her clothes and goes back to Alexine's, who gives her a meager meal and puts her to work with raw wax. For days, or maybe weeks, we stay with Lily as she repeats a grueling loop of activities: wake up, make the bus, get through the day hungry, go to Alexine's, go home, go to bed; repeat; repeat; repeat.

Lily learns quickly, with Alexine standing over her, how to refine wax, make salves, cap jars of honey and preserves, and boil it down for candlesticks. When the girl makes the slightest mistake, Alexine berates her. When the girl burns herself on hot wax, Alexine calls her clumsy and plunges her hand violently into a pail of cold water. She tells her to go home if she's too tired to work today.

Lily sobs. You take out a wad of your dispatches to dry her tears. We're shocked and dismayed to see Alexine behave like this.

It prompts me to pull out that old DISCONTINUED dispatch from my satchel, rip off the pink copy, and post it on her door. There's a pall over the whole operation now.

The dispatch does nothing to ease Lily's situation. It's no wonder the girl cries herself to sleep at night.

One night, Jack comes to her bedroom door and says, "Hey kid, are you crying?"

Jack finds out what's been going on, and he's mad. It's after dark, but he's going to Alexine's to have it out.

Something in me is paralyzed. I cannot follow. You remind me that this may be a good juncture to change the story from a tragedy to one that can reclaim the future. Simply tweek it at a key moment such as this. I feel strongly, I can feel it, that this may be such a place.

Chapter 41: Raging Bonfire

Lily doesn't let Jack go without her.
She's going with him.
We four go through the woods to Alexine's. On
approach, we come upon a roaring bonfire and
the figures of Alexine, Earl, and Duke beside it.
Jack stops in his tracks and grabs Lily's arm to
stop her from going further.

We all stop, and the woods are quiet without
the kids' footsteps in the fallen leaves. The only

sound is a chilly wind in the trees. Jack raises his index finger to his lips and whispers, "Shhhh."

Alexine and Earl are arguing, that's for sure. She screeches and howls, stabbing a large stick toward him in accusation. We catch the end of what she says, "... after all I've done for you!"

Duke is ill at ease, standing on all fours with his ears up facing Earl.

Alexine stokes the fire with the stick and sends sparks up into the clear night sky. Her gray hair sticks out and flows over a shawl and down her back.

The wind shifts and blows smoke toward Earl on the other side of the fire pit. He waves his hand and moves into the shadows, toward us! We can see him open his fly and pee.

Jack and Lily watch transfixed as Alexine holds up the stick and turns her face to the moon. She closes her eyes. She mumbles something inaudible. From up the hill, it sounds like an incantation. She reaches her free hand up into the darkness and calls out.

Earl paces back like a four legged animal up on two feet. He gets more logs from the pile and tosses them into the flame. He empties a bottle of booze into his upturned mouth and tosses it into the fire. Duke barks at Earl.

"I'm outta here, y'old hag," he says, turning to walk away.

"I know where you're goin' you bastard,"
Alexine says. She points the stick across the
street toward Veronica's and Darla's house. "Go
on to your little whorehouse where you belong."

This is an ugly side of the woman that escapes
her when she drinks.

Earl grunts something back in a low voice.
He waves off Alexine and walks away, gets in his
truck, and peels down the driveway. He crosses
Sumditch Avenue toward Florence's house.

Jack marches toward the fire pit. Lily catches
up to him and pulls at his sleeve, but he pulls his
arm away and keeps walking. Lily follows, and so
do we.

Alexine stands still as a statue beside the fire
pit, and when Duke hears us approaching his
ears perk up. He runs toward us barking and
snarling. He soon realizes it's the Bogle kids and
breaks into a happier gait. When he gets to Lily,
his tail is wagging. Jack pats him on the back.
"Good boy, Duke," Jack says.

When we all reach the fire pit, Jack says, "We
need to talk."

Alexine stares blankly at the kids. She calls
Duke to her side, "Duke! Come'ere ya stupid
mutt."

"Two things," Jack says. "One, you owe my
sister money and we need it now. Two, you owe
my sister an apology for how you've been treating

her. She just told me everything that's been going
on over here lately."

Alexine thinks about that for a long minute.
"Well I've got two sings, too. Two, too," Alexine
says, counting her own index and middle
fingers, wagging them in the air. Big flames feed
hungrily along the contours of the logs. Her eyes
are glazed, and the orange fire is reflected in
them. "One, one! I don't owe you anything! No,
nothhing. You! You owe me. And two, you two
derelickks are trespassissing on myyy property.
Get out!"

Jack glares at Alexine and says in a low voice,
"You go in the house right now and get what you
owe her."

"It's okay, Jack!" Lily says and pulls on Jack's
sleeve. "Let's just get out of here."

"Yes, leave!" Alexine says and wields her stick
violently in the air in their direction.

Duke barks wildly at her. She tells him to be
quiet. He barks louder.

Jack pulls his sleeve away from Lily and points
to the ground with his index finger. "Now!"

Faced with the three of them against her,
Alexine throws her stick into the fire, turns and
stomps toward the house. The kids and Duke
follow her.

Alexine goes in the back door of the house and
turns on the lights in the kitchen. She comes to

the back door and throws a few bills outside. She says, "Don't ever come around here again! Duke, come!"

Duke goes inside with his tail between his legs, and Alexine slams the door shut, narrowly missing his hind quarters.

Jack and Lily collect the bills.

"I'm going across the street. You go on home," Jack says to Lily.

"I'm not walking back home through the woods at night by myself!"

"Fine," Jack says.

The two walk down Alexine's driveway and across Sumditch Avenue. They walk past the Dempsey's corn field, all picked over by the farmers and then the birds and other critters. The stalks look like ragged soldiers in a ghost army.

All the lights are on in the cottage.

The headlights of Earl's truck illuminate the driveway and back yard. We come upon quite a scene.

Chapter 42: Jack to the Rescue

We arrive on the scene to find Earl walking Veronica and Darla toward the truck, with Florence pulling at him from behind.

Darla doesn't seem to want to go. She tries to pry Earl's grip off of her wrist, screaming. "Get off! Get off me!"

"She doesn't have to come!" Veronica screams at Earl. "Just leave her alone!" Veronica says to Earl.

Jack says, "Hey! What's going on?"

Florence runs up behind Earl and pounds her fists on Earl's back to no effect, so she pulls at the back of his shirt. He shoves her to the ground and keeps walking to his truck, ushering Veronica in front of him. Darla screams at Veronica to come back as she clings to her mother on the ground. Earl shoves Veronica into the driver's side of the truck and tells her to push over. She does what he says.

Darla runs up to the truck and screams at Veronica to get out. Earl reaches for Darla and easily picks her up and puts her in the truck beside Veronica, then gets in.

Jack heads toward the driver side of the truck.

Lily runs to stand in front of the truck, yelling at Veronica and Darla to get out. Her small figure is illuminated, and just her head is visible in front of the hood of the truck.

Veronica doesn't budge, and Earl puts one foot on the brake and puts the engine in drive. Jack sees Earl do this and sees his sister standing in the headlights of the truck.

"Stop! My sister is in front of the truck!" Jack screams at Earl.

From where Earl sits high up in his seat, the fact is that he barely sees Lily and doesn't hear her screaming over the roar of the engine. He's drunk, we can smell his breath. His eyes are glassy.

He doesn't see her.

He can't see her.

He's going to run her over!

"No!" Jack yells furiously at Earl to shut the engine and for Lily to move from out in front of the damn truck!

Earl puts the truck in park and opens the truck door. Getting out, he elbows Jack in the face.

Earl yells, "Back away from the truck!" Lily stands frozen in place. Everyone yells all at once. Florence scoops Lily up and takes her over to the passenger side window where they resume begging Veronica and Darla to get out of the truck.

Earl gets back into the truck and revs the engine. He hollers for everyone to get out of his damn way. One hand grips the wheel and the other his gear shift.

Jack says calmly to Veronica, "Come on, get out of the truck for a minute."

"Just leave us alone, Jack! It doesn't concern you!" Veronica yells.

Jack climbs back up to try to shut the engine off again, saying calmly to Earl, "Turn the truck off for a minute. Get out. Let's talk about this, this is big trouble. This is like kidnapping. You're drunk and in no condition to drive."

Earl revs the engine again.

Jack climbs down, opens the door and reaches in to pull Earl out. Earl pushes Jack away and gets out on his own volition. Now he stands facing Jack. He looks Jack up, down and sideways. He snorts.

"Git on home, Jew boy," Earl says and spits with so much alcohol on his breath that a lighter could set it on fire.

Jack stands his ground. He looks like he's getting ready to tackle Earl if he has to.

Earl winds up and tries to sucker punch Jack, but Jack easily dodges him. Earl loses his balance. When he looks back up, Jack is standing between him and his truck. Swaying, he wipes his hands on his pant legs and lumbers back toward his truck, shoving Jack. "Not messing around with you, ya little prick." Earl holds onto the door as he climbs into the driver's seat. As Earl fumbles to pull the door closed, Jack reaches up and pulls him back out of the truck.

"Jack, just let us go!" Veronica yells. "You don't understand! Jack!"

Jack jams his foot into one of Earl's knees, and Earl cries out, losing his balance, and almost going down. He stands back up as straight as he can. With a limp, he goes after Jack, swinging at his face. But Jack easily dodges Earl's heavy movements. Earl makes like he's going to just walk around Jack, but Jack pushes him away from the truck. In the tussle, Earl sneaks a punch into Jack's belly. Jack doubles over.

Florence tries to pull Earl away, and he shoves her to the ground. With Jack struggling to get his breath back, Earl goes to the bed of his truck. He rummages around for something, clunking metal and wood against the metal truck bed. Jack delivers a running kick to the backs of both of Earl's knees, and Earl falls down the side of the truck. When he sits up and turns around, he's got a tire iron in his left hand. He switches it to his right hand, gets up, and circles around Jack.

Florence screams. Veronica gets out of the truck and runs around to the other side. She and her mother stand screaming at Earl and Jack to stop. Lily latches onto Earl's free hand, screaming and crying for Earl not to hurt Jack.

Earl is momentarily stopped in his tracks at Lily's tears, and Jack takes the opportunity to throw dirt at Earl's face. Earl swings wildly with the tire iron at where Jack's head would have been. Jack kicks Earl hard in the nuts. Earl folds, dropping the iron. Jack kicks the tire iron away and kicks Earl in the face. Earl goes into a fetal position with one hand on his groin and the other around his head. Jack picks up the tire iron and stands over Earl breathing hard.

Earl groans and curses, then he growls and cackles like a mad man. "You prick!" Earl says in a high pitch voice. He starts to get up. Jack kicks him hard in the ribs, over and over again. Earl goes back into the fetal position and lays quietly.

Florence and Veronica pull Jack away from Earl.

"That's enough!" Florence says.

Jack walks up to the side of the truck, takes out his pocket knife and punctures the soft front driver side tire. Then he does the rear driver side tire. Then the rear passenger side tire. Just as Jack slashes the front passenger side tire, Earl lifts his head and sees what Jack has done. He puts his head back down and lets out a strange, animal sound.

Veronica goes up to Jack and screams, "That's enough, Jack!"

They leave Earl in the driveway and go in the house. It gets quiet, and the lights go out.

Earl, still inebriated, gets up slowly. He gets a closer look at what Jack did to his tires, concentrating so hard that he drools a little. He picks up the tire iron and starts to change his tires. He soon realizes he doesn't have four spares, and in a tantrum, hits his shin with the sharp end of the tire iron. He cries out in pain.

Earl goes toward the house. He limps up the porch steps and tries the door. A girl screams inside, and he looks over and up at the windows. He tries the door, but it's locked. He pounds on the door. There's no reply. He pounds louder.

"Florence!" Earl steps back and peers into the window. "Florence! I'm hurt. Flo, please. Open the door. Let me in. I won't do anything!" He pleads desperately. "Florence, you whore, you bitch, you, you..., how could you do this to me?"

He turns and goes back to the truck. By the light of the moon, he fishes around and pulls out a fresh fifth of bourbon. "Little prick," he mutters to himself. "Damn whore."

He takes a long swig, puts the cap back on, and limps off with it toward his house, straight through the corn field.

Along the way, he trips and falls in the corn field. With difficulty, he gets up. When he falls again, he just sits there and doesn't try to get up. He squints his eyes, trying to recall something. He touches his leg and winces.

The light of the moon barely reaches down through the tall, dry stalks. Striations of light put Earl's face behind bars of shadow and light. He unscrews his bottle of booze and gulps down the rest, tossing aside the empty bottle. He lets himself fall onto his back. He closes his eyes. A cold wind blows through the stalks.

You cover Earl in dispatches from your satchel, and he falls into a deep sleep.

Chapter 43: Gruesome Discovery

Early the next morning, sirens pierce the gray brisk air.

A parade of the town's emergency vehicles — fire, ambulance, police and the auxiliary branches — scream down Sumditch Avenue and turn into the Dempsey driveway. All the traffic on Sumditch is stopped, turned back, on both sides.

What happened?

Grandma Dempsey is making coffee in the

large percolator. Old Man Dempsey is at the kitchen table with a blanket over his shoulders and a hot coffee in his hands. As many times as Old Man Dempsey repeats the story, repeating the same details, he can't believe it. He's stricken.

Visitors file in. It's quite a large gathering, with most seating in the kitchen, living room and dining room occupied.

We find Kevin and his father helping with the emergency personnel going back and forth between the barn and the corn field.

Gruesome is right, but here's the news clipping, which tells the whole story quite well:

GRUESOME FARM ACCIDENT
Local man killed; Police say no foul play

"This was an unfortunate accident involving two of our local farmers," said Police Chief Peter Hallock. "One of our local farmers, Earl Butts, died from wounds resulting from being run over by a plow. The plow was operated by Mr. James Dempsey, just before sunrise."

Mr. Dempsey, who said he started plowing before dawn because he couldn't sleep, started at the far end of the field so as not to wake anyone. He felt the tractor lurch over a large object.

"The moment I realized that I'd run someone over -- I couldn't tell who the man was -- I felt sick, like I was going to have a heart attack," Mr. Dempsey said. Mr. Dempsey, who is 82 years old, went back to the house on foot and called 9-1-1.

Help arrived to find the victim dead, slashed from head to foot, according to Fire Chief Dan O'Mally. "It was like something out of a horror movie. He died of his injuries at the scene of the accident."

Mr. Dempsey's son, Kevin Dempsey, Sr., said his father has pitched in a lot lately, especially with the drought conditions. "There was nothing unusual about him plowing at dawn, except that Mr. Butts was lying in its path. We're in shock, quite honestly, we all feel awful about it. We're deeply sorry for Earl's family."

I save the clipping in my satchel for the report.

There's traffic up and down Sumditch Avenue for days. People want to drive by the scene of the accident. Everyone's coming or going at the Dempseys' and Butts' farms.

In passing, we overhear some of what people are saying.

It was a horrifying scene, they say.

What a terrible, terrible way to go. The plow chewed him up and spit him out.

They had to put him in the ambulance in pieces.

Oh! No one can believe it; everyone is in

disbelief.

His poor family, what it's been through, now this!

Old Man Dempsey, he shouldn't be driving anymore, especially in the dark.

What in heck was Earl doing laying in the middle of the corn field anyway?

Drunk, out cold, they say.

He was walking home from his girlfriend's house. There was some kind of trouble over there the night before.

Why didn't he just drive home? Why was he walking? Where was his truck? He's always in his truck.

It's over at her house for some reason. Probably because he was drunk and couldn't drive.

His truck tires were flat as pancakes, slashed!

That kid, the reporter's son, I heard he was the one who slashed Earl's tires.

Slashed the tires and rang his bell, too!

Maybe he gave Earl a concussion.

Earl was over at the old Hag's, too, drinking. They had one of their knock down drag out fights.

So Earl just drank too much, had a big fight with his girlfriend, and passed out in the corn field?

Someone I know who was on the scene said you could smell the alcohol, and there was an empty bottle of booze broken open right there next to Earl's severed arm.

I take notes furiously and file them as dispatches in my satchel, one after the other.

We follow a trail of people, including the pastor, to the residence of the Butts family. We're ushered through the hall and into the kitchen where Mr. and Mrs. Butts and their crippled son — so much heartache in the Butts family — sit staring vacantly at the center of the table.

The pastor walks the family through the rites, reassures them of life everlasting, and leads a prayer asking for God's mercy and care. In a while, the pastor gets up to go, leaving the family in much the same way as he found them: forsaken.

"You will all be reunited in Heaven, Mrs. Butts, take heart," he says as he leaves.

Mrs. Butts is unresponsive.

You pull out a dispatch and create a condolence card expressing our remorse and regret for Earl's untimely death. We both sign it and leave it in a basket in the hall on our way out.

In my mission report to the Org, I may tone down the carnage of that plow accident. It may be overly gruesome. But I'll tell you what, accidents with farm equipment is a leading cause of death in the agricultural sector. It's perfectly plausible.

After the accident, traffic on Sumditch Avenue

winds down to its quiet winter pattern. Indeed, the horrific death refreshes the town's idea of the twisted road as one to avoid.

Part IV: Winter

Chapter 44: A Bridge Appears

With Earl's untimely death, it's as if someone has flipped a switch.

We catch up with Jack riding his bicycle around town. He's looking for work.

The grocery store offers him a job stocking shelves and bagging groceries. Jack takes it. The bicycle shop needs a repair guy, and Jack takes that job, too. He'll be working after school and on weekends.

With his first paychecks, Jack buys groceries.
When he gets home with them, he goes into
Hannah's darkened room and gives her most
of the rest of his money. "Here, Mom," he says,
putting the bills on her dresser. "I'm gonna get
dinner going."

Lily comes into the kitchen, barraging him
with questions: what he got, where he'd gotten it,
what he was doing. He stocks the cupboards and
fridge and starts cooking.

"Alright," Jack says. "Here ya go, start with
this." He sits her down at the table with a glass
of milk and corn chips while he slices potatoes
and gets them frying in a pan with oil and salt
and pepper. He asks her if she has homework.
She recites a list of her assignments, practically
singing it. But, she says, she's already done it.

He says, "That's my girl."

He cracks eggs into a bowl. He adds a splash
of milk and a pinch of salt and scrambles them.
When a second pan is hot, he adds a pat of butter
and melts it all over the bottom of the pan. He
pours the scrambled eggs in, drains a can of peas,
and sprinkles the peas in the eggs. He flips the
potatoes in the other pan and puts out paper
napkins on a plate. As the eggs cook and set, Jack
scrapes the bottom of the pan, letting uncooked
egg ooze onto heat. He does that until the pea-
green-speckled curds of egg are cooked. He turns

off the heat under the eggs.

When the potatoes are fork tender, he removes them from the pan onto the paper towels. He sprinkles salt and pepper on them.

He gets out three plates, utensils, and ketchup and sets them on the kitchen table.

"Mom! Dinner's ready," Jack calls into Hannah's room.

Lily skips into Hannah's room and comes right back to the table. Hannah follows slowly behind, her eyes adjusting to the kitchen light from the darkness. Jack piles eggs, then potatoes on the plates.

Everyone eats hungrily and quietly. Lily doesn't like canned peas, but today they're delicious in eggs. The potatoes are out of this world.

"This is delicious," Hannah says. "Tell me about your new job."

"Jobs, plural," Jack says.

The very next day, while the Bogle kids are at school, Francesca stops by with a coffee cake. Hannah answers the door with a blanket wrapped around her shoulders.

Francesca comes into the kitchen and fishes in her bag for an envelope. She pushes it over to Hannah's side of the table. "It's the money you lent me," Francesca says. "Thank you again, it was a lifesaver."

"Oh, thank you, we could sure use it now."

"Plus I added extra because I want to commission a painting, if you would agree to it," Francesca says.

"A painting?" Hannah says. She stands at the sink, the fire under the kettle, wrapping her blanket around herself. She looks haggard. Her hair is a mess.

"Here, you sit down, and I'll do that," Francesca says, swapping places with her friend. As she gets coffee ready and plates slices of cake, she talks about the painting. "Well, I thought of you immediately. I'm actually very excited about it. Kevin and his dad came up with new ideas for the farm. Things that would make more money than corn and potatoes without killing ourselves."

"Drugs?"

"Ha!" Francesca laughs. "No, silly, a nursery. Ya know, flowers, shrubbery, small trees and that sort of thing. We're even looking into sod."

"Sod? That's the lush green grass they roll up and sell as ready-made lawns?" Hannah says.

"Yes."

"And that's more profitable?"

"Yes, a lot more. It's hard to compete on vegetables these days. But landscaping, that's a whole different story. And there's a farmer up the road putting in grape vines to make wine! Can you imagine?"

"My goodness!" Hannah says, watching Francesca put out the cups and silverware, sugar, milk, and the jar of instant coffee.

"Kevin wants me involved in sales, starting with me pictured on their best signature products."

"How lovely!" says Hannah. "What will the signature products be?"

"We don't know yet. We have to figure everything out. The state is buying a strip of our land along the road for them to extend the highway someday. We'll be able to invest in some new equipment and take some time to try out some new crops. The more we talk about it, the more ideas we get."

"How exciting! I have no doubt it will be a great success," Hannah says awestruck. "So they're going ahead with that bridge, huh?"

"Well, maybe someday. Alexine's still a holdout but they might be able get around her. She's a hoot!"

"What about the Butts, didn't Earl sell the whole farm?"

"Yes, that's apparently in process, and the Butts family is moving away," says Francesca. She points to the envelope. "By the way, the portrait commission money in the envelope is just a downpayment. Whatever it costs, let me know."

"Thank you," Hannah says, picking up the envelope and holding it to her heart. "The commission is a godsend, and actually, I would truly love to do a portrait of you."

They jabber on until the words are all said. And then they eek out more anyway. They part with a few more words.

After Francesca leaves, it's quiet. Hannah goes back into the kitchen and clears up the coffee and cake. She puts the envelope on her dresser in her bedroom.

Just then, the phone rings, "Brinnggg!" It's Dylan calling.

"They offered me a job back at the paper, the one where I used to work. It's only on the delivery truck until they have an opening on the news desk. It's not much money, but I can find more work. I think I should take it, don't you? The only trouble is I may not be able to be home much until we get things figured out."

"And I could always find something, too," Hannah says.

"I have news on that front, too. I showed your slides to some galleries downtown, and there's definitely interest. Ya know, the city has a whole new feeling than when we left. I'm kind of excited about moving back."

"That sounds wonderful, Dylan," Hannah says

and starts to cry. "It's been pretty cold and bleak
out here lately."

"I know, I know. Okay, so I'll take the job
then," Dylan says. "I start at two in the morning,
so I'd better find a room, get something to eat,
and get some sleep."

Hannah hangs up and gazes at a ray of winter
sunshine coming in the doorway.

Dylan doesn't get home for weeks on end, and
the Bogles carry on through the winter. It's not
a renaissance period, but it does feel like a quiet
reformation.

One late winter day, Dylan returns from a stint
in the city, a Friday night, and he and Hannah
shut themselves in their room. They talk into the
night. The next day, they tell the kids it's time for
the whole family to move back to the city.

Even before the school year ends, the Bogles
hit the road. Dylan pulls out of the driveway
with no hesitation or sentimentality. Sumditch
Avenue disappears out of the rear view mirror.

Dylan and Hannah talk with that far away look
on their faces. Lily tries to listen but can't hear
with the back windows open all the way. Jack
doesn't care what anyone says, sitting there with
his hand out the window, wind in his hair, and
the world whizzing by.

I take one last look at the Bogles in that
moment. Together, they came out of their island

years, and now they're happily off on a new adventure. As they drive away, I'm having a feeling, a very strong feeling. I let tears come to my eyes and fall down my cheeks. I take out the last dispatch -- "NEW LEASE" -- from my satchel and wave it in the air to wish them well and to say goodbye. I release it and watch it float in the air currents onto the double yellow lined road. You take out your last dispatch and offer it to me to wipe my tears. We stand there as the car drives into the distance and disappears from view.

I get an incoming message. It's from TS: "STAND BY FOR EXTRACTION PLAN."

I show this to you, and we're both elated. A second message comes in: "MEET SEAPLANE OFFSHORE DEAD END BEACH 14:00."

We hitch a ride to the end of the island, to our Dead End beachhead and arrive in the nick of time. We see a seaplane bobbing off the coast. Our pockets buzz with so many points that I'd worry about it except that they weigh nothing.

The surf's up as we wade in, diving under the steadily incoming waves. We make it past the breakers to the waiting plane.

Without delay, we buckle ourselves in and take off into the sky. Looking out the window as the island below grows smaller and smaller, we can't help but feel exuberant again.

I turn to you with a big smile on my face. High

five for mission accomplished and dispatches delivered!

We gain altitude and view the Outer Lands Archipelago below. The GPS display on the Org app, which is fully functional now, shows a graphic map of our flight from the island over the sea to the mainland airbase. The route, which is a digital rendering made of light waves, appears as a golden yellow bridge.

There's our bridge! We marvel at it. Though not the material we expect, it is instantly recognizable as the very symbol of our quest for a bridge to the future.

I get a message: "CONGRATULATIONS! You have successfully completed your mission! Based on your 50,000+ points balance, you're eligible for our NEXT WAVE tier of options for your next mission with the Org. Please click HERE to browse now!"

I'll browse later. Right now I call TS. He finally, actually gets on the line. It's wonderful to talk to him again, but I must admit to feeling a bit sour. I ask him whether he and my ex-therapist coordinated to get me back to my family's island years.

He denies it and says, "Things just have a way of coming back again and again in different ways until you go through them, Lily."

"Well, if it weren't for the Ink Drinker, I don't

think I would have ever made it out of there. As it was, I had to change the story, an idea the Ink Drinker had."

Pairing the Clerk with the Ink Drinker was his idea, TS says.

I started to wonder if I would have a problem with TS. He wasn't accessible during the whole mission. It was only after I and the Ink Drinker worked through it ourselves that we were able to reach him. Now here he is taking credit. Typical.

He asks when I'd have the mission report.

"It shouldn't take long, it's just a matter of putting all my dispatches together into one coherent document. The sooner it's off my plate, the better. Then I'm free once and for all."

Which mission will I choose next, TS asks.

"I have to think about it. I'm not at all sure when I'll be ready to hop onto another mission."

"Well," he says, "Hop on one sooner than later. In a choice between a new enlightenment and doomsday, the world seems to be leaning toward the latter. In fact, this new regime is hunting down people for their point of view and shipping them off to God know where, never to be seen or head from again."

"Really? That's terrible!" I promise to let him know my selection soon.

It's quite terrible, he continues. He knows a lot of people who are so scared of what the new

regime is doing that they've gone into hiding.
The Org can keep me out of harm's way until
things turn around, which they always do. "About
the report, though," he says. "The Org usually
distributes mission reports widely, but from what
I've seen from your dispatches, it may keep the
Outer Lands Mission Report under wraps. The
regime might take issue with it."

Why would they take issue with it? I'm
incredulous, and I listen carefully to his answer.

He says, "Well, let's see. It assassinates the
character of a very powerful figure. It brutally
slaughters a native son. It allows troublemakers
to escape unscathed. The story contains factually
incorrect things, and although authors have
had license to do that kind of thing in the past,
there are now crimes on the books under the
Publications Clause of the new Disinformation
Act. Stories must conform to a view that
recognizes and celebrates the triumph of power
and privilege. Giving false hope to people who
would challenge the status quo is considered
seditious. At a minimum, the regime could ban
the report. At worst, press charges."

"You've got to be kidding," I say. "That's
absurd. Well, I'd like the report to be made
available in case it could help anyone else. I'll be
fine."

We agree to check back in soon and hang up.

When we land at the airfield, you and I thank the pilot and prepare to part ways. Returning to base on the mainland, we're struck by the gap in so-called progress compared to the archipelago. The islands lag by 50 years or more! Seasons turn, the tides come and go, and the Outer Lands Archipelago holds its power.

As we walk to the tower, you ask what happened to Alexine, the Dempseys, the two sisters, the town? Did they ever build the bridge? Does One get to look at it from his window?

My mother kept in touch with Francesca and got all the gossip. Alexine fell off a ladder at her farm and died of complications from that. Apparently she sold the development rights on her farm to the county. It can only be used for farming or educational purposes. She donated the proceeds to several local groups working to preserve the agrarian way of life for posterity.

Her sale of the farm's development rights threw a wrench in plans for the bridge, but it gets floated every once in a while. Miraculously, the island has largely remained agricultural all these years into the quantum age! It's a kind of new rural age. People really love visiting, and real estate is booming. Everyone wants water views, and everyone connects very strongly with the land and the seasons! Her property is now a museum they call Twisted Hollow Farm because of how Sumditch Avenue twists and turns at that spot in the road and because of her otherworldy reputation. They do a major Halloween fundraising event there every year to keep the place going. It turns out that people really love to be in such a terribly beautiful place, and for now they don't want it destroyed by a commercial highway and bridge.

The Dempseys are still out there on the island, their family is growing, and their nursery business is booming. The sisters, Veronica and Darla, babysat for Francesca, then got involved in the Dempsey's new farming operation there. They're doing very well!

The Butts family, as you know, sold the farm and moved away.

DEAD END beach is still a dead end, and the sign is a triumph over the highway extension and bridge proposal.

No, One never got to see that bridge from his window, and not only because of Alexine's land preservation deal. One and Steve went to jail for fraud and human trafficking after police raided one of their more obscene parties. Another very good reporter did a full expose. It made national news. Far from transcending the human condition, the duo landed in a particularly low place indeed.

We enter the air tower, and you ask about the

Bogles and what became of us all.

My parents and I moved back into the city.

You're a bit confused.

Yes, just my parents and I. During the mission, I changed the story from a tragedy to a happy ending. Earl isn't the one who died, it was actually my brother. What really happened that night was that Jack tried to save me from being run over. I was running home as fast as I could to get my parents, in the dark, by myself. I guess Earl got his truck into gear and went flying down the driveway with my brother holding on. Jack lost his grip and went under the truck.

Good Lord!

He died that night. I changed the story to get through the mission and to rectify a gross injustice that was dealt by a random twist of fate. One small change in the story changed everything. Everything flowed from there. No one should have died that night, but if someone had to make a sacrifice, it could have been Earl.

My parents were never the same. Their hopes and dreams died with my brother, who was destined for great things. If anyone should have died it should have been me.

Since those island years, I've felt like I've been under a spell, paralyzed by fear and shame. I felt encased in honeycomb, embalmed with the salty sweetness of the Outer Lands, imprinted

by invisible mystical forces. Now, released, I feel
as innocent as a child in a world that wasn't of
my making. A great weight has been lifted. The
report will show that and justice will be restored.

My feelings have returned. I experience
life as it unfolds, not in the past and not in the
future. I'm not in my head so much as my heart,
in my body. I see more clearly without all of
the distortions of other people's wars, beliefs,
judgments and illusions. It's quite a feeling!
What about you, Ink Drinker? What comes next
for you?

You'll continue helping to build bridges, you
say. Human consciousness is a strong filament
for powerful structures that can withstand the
test of time. You say it's been a pleasure to serve
with me, and it was quite an adventure.

With a salute, you wish me well.

I salute you. Thank you for your service, you're
a true hero. It would be an honor to serve with
you again someday.

Good luck and Godspeed.

We exit the tower.

THE END

Acknowledgments

In the words of rapper Snoop Dog, "I would like to thank me." Wait! I know that sounds bad, and I do have many acknowledgements right after this. Thank you for indulging me.

My first, this novel took ten years to write, on and off. I had so many epiphanies in the process that they amounted to a personal enlightenment. Too early, I asked a few friends and relatives to read it, thereby destroying their will to read. I edited the whole thing so many times that I lost count. I strained most of my relationships to the brink. In order to keep going, I took up acrylic painting as art therapy and made a series of illustrations to go with it. The layout and design phase was yet another chance to edit.

Why? What was so important?

I can't throw away that much work and have nothing to show for it. Also, stories and art have power and justice. By reading *The Clerk and the Ink Drinker in the Outer Lands Mission,* you helped complete a circle. I must thank YOU, the Ink Drinker!

After me and you, other acknowledgments are not the usual cast of characters for a project like this, such as publishers, editors, designers, and publicists.

First and foremost I thank my husband and children for their support, encouragement and understanding. They're my biggest fans.

I thank my parents for giving me the gift of art and literature as well as an appreciation of current events. I thank one grandmother for being my best pen pal and the other for teaching me commerce, driving and community theater. I thank my friends and family for hanging in there through my coccoon and caterpillar stages. Ha! All that and I'm just a moth!

Thank you to my fellow creatives who shared

their own crazy journeys with me and inspired me to keep going. Thank you to those who I asked for creative input and who gave me so many great ideas.

I thank my schoolteachers and professors, online course teachers and tutorial givers. I thank my bosses, clients, colleagues and fellow citizens for their high standards and support. I even thank my enemies, haters and doubters for giving me something to prove. Everyone we meet has impact.

I wouldn't even try to name everyone, but I am incredibly grateful to all, and you know who you are. Thank YOU!

The Author & Painter

N.G. Swett lives in the Outer Lands Archipelago, East Coast, New York, USA. She lives with her husband and has two grown children. She graduated from Stuyvesant High School in New York City. She studied political science at the State University of New York at Binghamton and at Sciences Politiques in Paris, France. She owns her own communications company and is an advocate for families, downtown revitalization, and shelter pets.

4seasonshelf.com

N.G. Swett's books, artworks, and sundries
are available at 4seasonshelf.com, along with her
blog, free enewsletter, and contact information.

Illustrations

*The acrylic paintings and black & white graphics from this novel (see page numbers below for reference) may be available as originals or prints at **4seasonshelf.com**:*

Also by N.G. Swett

Available
Internationally